P9-EEM-043

THE HUNTER

THE

ROBERT HOLLAND

HUNTER

STEIN AND DAY/*Publishers*/New York

The characters and occurrences herein are fictional, and not intended to portray any real persons or events.

First published in 1971

Library of Congress Catalog No. 73-160355

Published simultaneously in Canada by Saunders of Toronto Ltd.
Designed by David Miller
Printed in the United States of America
Stein and Day/Publishers/7 East 48 Street, New York, N.Y. 10017
ISBN 0-1828-1411-8

THE HUNTER

1

LEAVING HOME WAS the easiest thing Billy Oakes had ever done. He rolled out of his narrow bed in the barn one morning three hours before the sky had begun growing light in the east and walked away from the house he had been born in and where his sister and mother were still sleeping.

He took some dried venison from the kitchen and walked down to the railroad siding where the northbound freight idled against the night as the passenger express from Charlotte flashed past, parting the damp darkness in high, rolling waves.

It was still dark and cold with the smell of spring running close to the ground. He slipped under the car and, finding the thick steel brake rods, slung himself over them, his back to the ground. When the freight pulled back onto the line, Billy crossed out of Georgia while the tapering ridges of the Great Smokies that had framed his entire life brooded unseen on both sides of the train.

He was headed north to where New York was supposed to be and where his cousin lived in a place called Lakeport.

He had seen men riding this way, flashing past him as he stood by the tracks, and it had looked easy enough for them, draped over the thin metal shafts, skimming scant inches above the stone and cinders, but he had not figured on the sound and the first time the train roared over a crossing at high speed, the sudden noise nearly made him let go.

And in the curves the wheels threw sparks back at him, lighting and dying on his clothes as the pressure of the banked curve pushed his body against the rods.

When he skinned out from under the car in the yards at Charlotte, North Carolina, the backs of his denim jacket and blue jeans were covered with gray dust except for the two strips which had been protected by the rods. Even the backs of his boots had gone gray from the flying dust. He whacked most of it off, slapping the loose material at the backs of his legs and then pulling off his jacket and pounding the dust out of the back. His arms and legs ached from the strain of having had to hold so tightly to the train, and he knew he would have to find a car he could get inside. Riding under the cars that way would tire him out, and he was afraid he would just slip off beneath the wheels.

The day was bright, full and summer-lush the way the spring days sometimes come on in the South, rich and yellow even as the clouds build steadily on the horizon before finally spilling the steady rain.

Billy began looking for another car, and if he was aware of the danger from railroad cops he did not show it, walking casually along, looking at each car.

Climbing between two of them, he noticed a paper tag stapled to the end. He could read enough to make out that the tag gave the destination of each car. It took nearly an hour to find one marked for Lakeport, and he had to force the lock to get in.

The car was full nearly to the roof with big rolls of paper. He climbed to the top and settled in, draping his five feet eight inches like a hammock over one of the rolls, with his shoulders and head against the end wall of the car. He slept soundly, not moving until the car was rammed backward by the yard engine as it picked up his car and then rammed it into another car. Only Billy's eyes moved, snapping open, immediately clear and free from the hazy sheen of sleep.

The clicking wheels and the howls of the wheel flanges on the corners rocked him into drowsiness, and he lay with his eyes half open thinking about his home and his family and his father serving life in the big prison in Atlanta. Sticking Bob Perkins was what had got him caught. Everybody knew who had done it and they knew it was because of Billy's sister. After they took his father off to prison his mother kept them in store food by going with some of the men from the town, and his sister helped out too. At seventeen she was pretty, not as pretty as his cousin Daniel's wife Sarah Ann, but she had bigger tits and thin hips and nobody who came to the house seemed to notice too much else.

Often when Billy had come back from hunting with his hounds, his sister would come and climb into bed with him and he would have to sleep late the next morning.

It was not until he had turned sixteen that he began making nightly trips to her bed, seeking the warmth of her body and the release. By the end of that summer, the same one that Daniel had left in, Billy stopped going and she no longer came to him. He hated her worse then than he had when he was a little boy. After the leaves had begun to fall he went back to hunting as his father had taught him, with his dogs and his rifle, walking off into the tall hills and the trees for weeks at a time, living off what he could kill.

He thought back to the day he had decided to leave. The air had been sharp for spring, almost more like fall as he sat on the top of Goose Creek Mountain looking out across the valley, over the tops of the trees. There wasn't any reason for staying, he had decided, except that he had never thought about leaving. Once he made up his mind, it was only a month before he was gone.

It took the car a week to get to Lakeport, and with his supply of dried meat gone, he was hollow with hunger.

After the car was switched off onto a siding, Billy tried to sleep, but the constant smell of fire, even though it was not close, made him uneasy. He could see clearly in the dark car and he purposely did not look directly into the bright light, blinding where it bled through the cracks in the door.

He was used to the smell of the paper now, and over it he could smell the fire. It was not like the fires back home, but stinging and sharp and it hurt his nose and the back of his throat. He wanted to get out of the car. But the wind, whistling soft and steady through the cracks in the walls, told him it was in the open and he would have to wait until dark.

Several hours passed and Billy slept. He did not sleep the way most people do, unaware of what is happening around them, but recording the approach and departure of sound, of changes in the wind, of the fire's nearness.

He snapped awake with the hard jamming lurch of the car as it was picked up by a switch engine. The sound inside the car was different now, and it was hard to hear the wheels of the car over the churning whine of the engine.

Then suddenly it was totally dark and it smelled dark and old and musty. He waited until they stopped, until the engine let go and pulled away with a sharp hiss.

When it was quiet, he slid down off the rolls to the door, opening it slowly into a dark tunnel. He climbed down out of the car and began walking back up the tunnel, his eyes already adjusted to the dark. The cinder floor was strewn with broken whiskey bottles and pieces of sodden paper, and the smell of water was overpowering. In several places Billy stepped around puddles kept full by a steady drip from the stone ceiling. Now the floor began to slant and Billy realized he was heading out, and then he could see the end arcing around the daylight, where the tunnel came out. He turned and walked back into the dark, back to where he had seen some crates and boxes. He piled them against the wall in a purposeful jumble and then crawled inside and went to sleep.

He awoke in the early morning, just on the dark edge of day. Now, trusting the darkness, he walked out, not even hesitating at the tunnel mouth. He followed the tracks and he could smell a dirty river off to his right and the sky behind him was bright with the glow of lights from the city. It smelled as if the whole place were on fire.

He rubbed his hollow, aching stomach, almost sure he could feel his backbone through the tight skin. In the mountains it would have been easy to find food, but here with the smoke obscuring the smells and no places for game to hide, he did not know where to begin and the fear of not knowing tightened his empty stomach into an angry ball. He stood perfectly still, not even blinking as he stared through the mist above the river.

Then suddenly he moved, exploding into a fast, quick-cadenced walk, his long strides eating up the rubble-covered ground along the tracks as he wound through the high-walled pit which led from the tunnel and up onto the embankment. Now he could see the river winding off away from him, hiding momentarily beneath bridges and then jumping out on the other side until he could not see the water and he knew there must be a dam. He did not like the smell of the river, thick like the juices that flowed out of his outhouse at home, but it was a good thing to remember because by walking in the shallow edges of the river he could keep away from the dogs if he had to run.

He stopped and looked back to where the tracks curved away to the left and went on under the river. His father would be no help to him now, except in the things he had told him. It would take all that and something more just to stay alive. He did not know how people lived here in this place with nothing to hunt, and without farms.

He turned and walked along the embankment to where it crossed beneath a road, climbed up the long, slanted concrete bulkhead to the top, turning then and moving away from the river. Somewhere off to his right he could smell some trees and he headed for them.

Mingled with the trees he could smell the sun still brooding below the horizon. The street he turned onto was deserted except for an occasional dashing rat or a cat or a dog hunting alone, skirting the sound of Billy's footsteps. He turned onto a side street, walking beneath a long double row of trees heavy with spring buds. He did not know where he was headed or what he was looking for until he saw the lights of an all-night grocery store on Alexander Street.

He walked in slowly, drifting toward the back of the store and then staying there until the clerk, a tall, skinny young man, grew curious and walked back to check. He saw Billy standing in front of the meat case.

"Need any help?"

Billy stared at him, unblinking and wary, but he did not answer. He did not know what to say.

"Is there anything you want?" The clerk waited again for an answer and when it didn't come he backed off a step. He was tired of working nights and having to deal with all the freaks that wandered in out of the dark. "Look, man," he said, "if you don't want anything, you'd better leave, huh?"

Billy stood with his shoulders slouched, trying to look casual in spite of the tension he could feel in his arms and in the backs of his thighs. He stood perfectly still, unable to predict the reaction to any move the clerk might make. The best thing was to wait.

The clerk stared into Billy's eyes, looking for signs that the kid might be tripping. He began to tighten up when he realized that the kid's eyes were normal.

"Hey, man," he said, "you were looking in the meat case, right? You want some meat?"

Billy nodded.

The clerk walked by him and around behind the case,

relieved to have some kind of barrier between them. You just never knew what was going to wander in after midnight. He thought about the knives behind him on the butcher's block, but he knew he could not use them. Once after reading about a guy getting his throat cut he had wondered what it would be like to kill a man with a knife and he had known he could not do it. He bent down and slid open the door of the meat case. "What kind do you want?" he asked.

Billy pointed to a thick steak.

The clerk pulled it out of the case and flopped it onto a piece of brown paper and then onto the scale. "That'll be three-fifty," he said.

Again, Billy just nodded. He had no money, but he knew the man was afraid of him. He could wait until they started toward the front of the store and then just grab the package and run.

But the clerk was wary, and after he'd wrapped the meat he motioned for Billy to go first toward the front of the store.

They were halfway down the aisle when Billy whirled around, his knife just a streak of silver in the fluorescent light. The big knife hit the clerk just under the chin and sliced halfway through his neck. Billy bent over him and used the clerk's apron to wipe off the knife, carefully cleaning around the hilt. He picked up the package and walked to the front of the store, and on the way out decided to take the cash from the register. He stood stuffing the bills into his pocket and looking back at the change, then decided to leave it there. It was too heavy and it would make too much noise.

Outside on the street again he walked quickly. He wanted to get as much distance between himself and that store as possible, but he did not dare run. It was a good thing he had killed the clerk. If he had taken the package and run, there would have been somebody behind him that knew what he looked like. And he smiled at having remembered to wipe off his knife the way his father had taught him. Dried blood was as easy to smell as fresh blood, and even a stray dog would give you away just by walking a wide circle around you.

Back in the tunnel he sat on one of the boxes and ate the big steak raw, cutting off small pieces with his knife. He chewed the bone absolutely clean and then worked out the marrow by sucking the bone. Finally, he tossed the naked bone across the tunnel for the rats.

He pulled a small whetstone from the top pocket of his denim jacket and began working it against the long blade, remembering the day his father had chopped the steel for it from an old, rusty cross-cut saw and filed it into shape. The handle had come from the antlers of the first buck deer Billy had killed, and the rough horn would not slip from his grasp even when he was gutting out a deer and it was wet with blood.

He spat on the metal and worked slowly, honing the thin blade and working carefully at the tip where it was rounded back for skinning. The knife was not a good sticking knife, because you had to push down and in, instead of just straight in.

The sheath was sewn into his shirt between his shoulder blades so that when the knife was tucked away the handle was just below the edge of his collar. He tested the edge of the blade by shaving off a small patch of hair, matted where he had spat on his arm. Satisfied, he slid his knife into the hard leather sheath and then hunched his shoulders several times in succession to make sure it lay flat, directly down the hollow of his spine.

When it was smooth and in place, he curled into a tight knot and slept until the bright daylight outside began pushing the thick spring warmth into the tunnel. He decided it was time to begin looking for his cousin.

Walking toward the bulkhead ramp outside, he was aware of a change in the sound. There were people talking as they walked by, and he had never before heard so many engines running at one time. He stopped at the bottom of the narrow gray concrete strip, looking up toward the bridge. He could see the people walking along casually and he felt as if he were standing at the bottom of a deep well, secure and protected, unwilling to climb out into the light. He hung his hands in his pockets, resting one foot on the ramp, shivering once as he thought of going up onto the bridge, of leaving himself without something solid behind him, of being surrounded.

With a sudden leap he started up the bulkhead, walking fast, his steps sure and light, knowing that once he hit the top he could not hesitate but would have to walk with the people.

He came up over the edge and stepped into the crowd. The noise was louder than a passing train. He had never seen so many cars, or known that they came so big and shiny. Back home those who drove anything drove trucks. He did not hesitate, but stayed with the flow of people passing on the sidewalk, his jaw muscles bunched tightly from the strain. The voices around him clacked like the edgy rankle of migrating blackbirds. He tried to listen to two women walking in front of him, but the conversation behind him drowned them out, and the heavy sweet smells from the women made him slightly sick.

When he followed them around a corner the wind was from a different direction and he picked up the odor of the men behind him, just as sweet and heavy as that from the women. He wondered whether it was the way they all smelled in the city or whether they could smell him, telling as clearly where he was from.

He walked along with the crowd, waiting for them to notice him by his smell or by the way he was dressed, but they did not and he began to relax. The sun was warm on his back.

Once he stepped off a curb into a puddle and glancing back noticed that the soles of his boots left a strange-looking mark. He stopped and checked the bottoms. There were holes the size of a quarter through each sole. He went into the first dry goods store he could find and stood looking at the pairs of boots lined up on the counter.

He picked a dark brown pair with smooth soles and took them up to the cash register in the front.

"You want to try them on?" the old man asked from behind the glass-topped counter.

"I reckon."

"From the South, huh?" The old man came around the counter and pointed toward a dark red chair.

Billy just nodded and looked down at the floor. He had not realized people here talked differently from the way he did, and it made him uneasy that his way of talking was picked up so easily by the first person he had said anything to.

"Well, you sit right over here, son, and we'll make sure those boots fit you right."

Billy slipped them on and laced them up, snug, but not so tight that they cut off the circulation.

"Gonna wear them?" the old man asked.

Billy nodded, standing and walking toward the counter. "How much?" he asked.

"Fifteen, plus tax."

He paid, carefully peeling the dollar bills off his roll.

"Hey," the man called as Billy started to leave. "Don't you want the old ones?"

"No," Billy said. He walked through the open door and into the crowded street.

As he walked he began to understand something about the city. People did not notice you. Even when they bumped into you, or walked into your path, they did not look but hurried on, seeing only ahead. By nightfall he was exhausted and his legs ached from walking on the hard pavement. He returned to the tunnel.

2

DANIEL HEWS sat with his short, heavy legs stretched in front of him, his heels propped on the shabby maroon ottoman in his living room, trying to concentrate on the evening newspaper while his two small towheaded kids moved over and under his legs in a chase so close it was impossible to tell the pursuer from the pursued.

It was hard enough to read without the kids hollering as they scooted under the bridge his legs formed between the chair and the ottoman. He had to read even more slowly, forcing himself through any sentences he did not understand.

He had never been to school, and the only reading he had been taught had come from a primer his mother had had before she married his father. Back in Georgia the little reading Daniel could do had been enough, maybe even too much. Here it wasn't enough to be worth anything.

He had gone as far as he could in his job at the plant without being able to read easily and well. When he came to words he didn't understand, he carefully marked them down in a small notebook. Later he would look them up in the dictionary his foreman had given him.

On Saturday afternoons he would go over the words he

had written down during the week, and on Sundays he would sit and memorize them.

At the bottom of the front page the small headline caught his eye. He read it slowly.

GROCERY CLERK MURDERED

George Bassat, 18, a student at the University of Lakeport, was found stabbed to death early this morning by a customer in the all-night grocery store on Alexander Street where Bassat worked as the night clerk.

Bassat, who comes from Chicago, was supporting himself here by working at the store. He also had a partial scholarship at the university.

Police said they have no clues to the killing.

Daniel looked away from the paper, suddenly bending it into his lap as his forehead furrowed with irritation. "Shut up!" he shouted at his kids. They froze, staring at him a long moment before tearing off toward the kitchen and their mother. Daniel straightened the paper with a quick, crinkling snap and read on.

The cash had been cleaned out of the register according to police, though some $25 in change was left untouched.

Police Chief Lemuel Barton said this morning that it did not appear to have been the work of a thief. He said the manager of the store, Fred Clark of 106 Tremont St., had told them that at most the register contained $30 in cash.

According to Detective Capt. James Ansella, who is conducting the investigation, the killer appeared to have wiped off his knife on the victim's apron before leaving.

Sarah Ann came into the living room and perched on the arm of the chair next to her husband. She touched her shiny blond hair where the strands stuck together in the moist heat of the room. The windows were closed against the spring dampness, and the room was warm with the furnace running for the first time in a month.

She had put on five pounds since they had come from Georgia two years ago, but all you could see of it was the small roll around her narrow waist, visible only because she had tucked her sweater into the tight waistband of her skirt.

"Don't shout so at the children, okay, honey?" she whispered.

He didn't answer, just sat staring at the blue wall peeling down to yellow and green.

"Honey?" she asked, her accent pulling at the words, stretching the soft syllables.

No answer.

"Daniel?" She leaned across in front of him, supporting herself on the opposite arm of the chair as she looked into his face. "Daniel, what are you thinking on so hard?"

"Huh?" He looked up at her, his eyes still blank. "Oh, nothing, I guess, just worried about my job."

She reached out and brushed his hair back off his forehead the way she always did to soothe him when he was discouraged.

He folded his hands in his lap and looked across at the wall again. "Well, I guess maybe I need some schooling or something, but there just ain't no time, not with all the overtime I got to work."

She swung around in front of him, sitting on his thighs and holding his broad face between her hands. "Honey, don't you worry. You'll find a way. Look how far we come since we left Georgia."

"Jesus, Sarah, that's just the point!" He twisted away from her hands and she dropped them into her lap. "We ain't come anywhere that I can see, living in a house full of niggers, surrounded by 'em, the kids playing with 'em. And if that ain't enough, every time we turn off the lights we got to worry about some damn junkie breaking in." He dropped his head back against the chair. "I work sixty hours a week and that just about pays for the rent and the food. Hell, maybe we oughta go back home."

"What did we have there? Trying to grow a few stinking vegetables, no schooling to speak of and we only got to town on Saturday, and when we got there we didn't have even one dime to spend." She stood up and walked across the living room, staring out through the slats in the venetian blinds. Now her voice was soft. "I'll tell you what I think, Daniel, I think it don't make no difference whether they're with niggers or not. At least our kids will go to school." She turned toward him. "All the time we was growing up I never seen you quit on anything, not in all them years. We got to start somewhere."

The frustration in her voice brought his head up and now he looked straight at her. She wasn't just trying to cheer him up, she meant it, and living like this had to be harder on her than it was on him. "I'm sorry, honey," he said. "I just get tired sometimes. Every day I got to learn about things I never heard of before. You know most any nigger you see has had more school than I have. Most of them can read more than me. Even the kids rattle me so I can't think."

She crossed back and sat on the edge of the ottoman, listening.

"You know," he said, "today a kid came into the shop looking for work. He'd been to high school and he went to trade school and, Sarah, I seen the foreman look around at me as he was talking to the kid and I know what he was thinking. He was thinking about firing me and giving the kid my job."

"He wouldn't do that."

"I think he would."

"But I thought the foreman was real high on you?"

"He is, I guess. I mean he give me them books and the dictionary, and he let me talk to some man in personnel about some kind of school the company is starting for men that didn't go to high school, but still . . . I just had this feeling."

"Can we come in now?"

Daniel and Sarah Ann looked toward the kitchen door at their two white-haired kids peeking around the door frame. Daniel smiled. "Sure, c'mon over here." They walked cautiously, not certain whether he had cooled down or not.

"It's okay," he said. "Daddy was just tired and he didn't mean to holler at you. You can play all you want."

Sarah leaned suddenly over and kissed him on the cheek, then whispered in his ear. "I love you more than anything," she said.

3

AFRAID NOW to ask questions because of his accent, Billy took three days of walking to find out where his cousin lived. He might never have found it if he hadn't asked a man in a gas station who looked it up in a book. And even then, knowing the name of the street and the number, it took most of another day to find Clarissa Street.

Now he walked along slowly, reading the numbers on the fronts of the shambled houses. He had never seen so many niggers. Where he had come from there was only one family of them besides the crazy woman who begged outside the bar. He hesitated only for a moment in front of Daniel's, resting his hand on the gray iron gate, and then walked on by.

Some of the people he passed wore their hair in shiny, slick-sided fashion and some just let it grow the way it usually did in tight, warm-looking curls that made Billy want to stick his hand in and wiggle his fingers.

Kids noticed him as he walked along, sometimes stepping lightly and quickly out of his way, sometimes making him walk around the spot on the sidewalk they had staked out for their games, but always looking at him, and he could imagine eyes in the dark faces behind the rotting porch railings staring out at him.

He picked up his pace, suddenly afraid of those eyes, seeing what other people would not. As he walked faster the noise from the children and the high-pitched laughter of the women rolled off the porches behind him and threatened to drown him in a crashing wave. And then he was running, fast and light as a rabbit, flying over the pavement looking for an opening across the street, a hole into which he could dive and hide.

When he spotted an alley with only a low fence at the end, he swerved across the street, just ahead of a truck, its brakes screaming. He cleared the low fence at the end of the alley and then tore down through the knee-deep grass in a vacant lot and toward the river and the railroad, stopping only when he had outrun the sound and then squatting deeply into the tall grass, listening for pursuers.

There were none. He stretched out and slowly caught his wind.

He lay there in the high, dry grass with a soft spring breeze waving the tops at him. A gust occasionally moved against his neck. Drowsing, soft sounds came out of his throat until he finally lay quietly, his breathing even and steady as a sun-snoozing dog.

When he woke it was dark. He sat bolt upright and looked around, then got up, shook off his clothes, and walked back up to Clarissa Street and back by his cousin's house. A police car slowed alongside him, but did not stop, and he kept on walking the street past the falling houses. Across from Daniel's there was an old house with the windows broken out and the door torn from its hinges. Billy walked around it and up onto the back porch, the old boards creaking under his feet. Except for the light which seeped in from outside, the house was dark. The front windows were tall and wide, and broad flashes of blue street light flooded across the rotting floor. Billy sat down by one of the windows and watched the house across the street.

He watched until midnight but did not see Daniel, only several niggers coming and going noisily, laughing and joking.

A very tall, broad-shouldered nigger turned in at the gate and walked on up to the front door, singing. What held Billy's attention was the way the man moved, lightly and easily for his size. The man opened the door and then slammed it shut so hard that he shattered the pane of glass. He did not stop but continued on up the stairs, Billy watching as his legs grew shorter with each step until he was out of sight. When he was gone, Billy left too and went back to the tunnel.

He did not mind the rats darting through the dark, occasionally clattering a piece of metal or broken glass on the cinder floor. Even now that he had food with him the rats did not come close to him, but shied away and around in the dark as he lay listening to them from behind the boxes and crates he had piled against the wall.

He was almost asleep when a new sound cracked through and he sat up quickly, reaching behind his neck for the knife, listening now, his breathing stopped as he strained to hear and see through the dark. Even before he saw the silhouette, he knew it was a dog. He could hear the characteristic, four-pawed meandering and sniffing. Billy stepped out from under the crates, crouched and ready as he watched the big animal move closer. The dog stopped and growled when he caught Billy's scent. Billy did not move, ready, poised to spring, not even blinking. Finally the animal retreated, his tail between his legs, fleeing from the scent.

As he drifted back toward sleep Billy thought about the big singing nigger that lived in Daniel's house. There was something in the way the man moved that made him seem dangerous. Anything that big that could move so light and easy was something to stay away from.

4

DANIEL WAS WORKING in the hall, putting up a new mailbox. It was the fourth this year. When he heard the singing outside he was sure it was the Smith guy who lived upstairs on the third floor. Mostly he wasn't any trouble, though when he got drunk he could make a lot of noise.

Daniel walked over and looked out through the new pane of glass he had installed before dinner. It was Smith all right and he looked pretty drunk, standing, fumbling with the gate latch, finally getting it open.

Daniel went back to working on the mailbox, listening to Smith's progress up the walk. He had just started the last screw when Smith opened the door and came in, stopping short as he saw Daniel.

"Hey there!" he shouted. "What're you doing?" He stopped as Daniel looked up. "Sorry," he said. "I thought somebody was busting into the mailboxes again. Couldn't see so good with only that one damn bulb."

"Sure makes it hard to see what you're doing," Daniel said.

"Yeah, sure does." Smith stood with his hands in his pockets watching as Daniel leaned against the screwdriver to set the screw. "You put the glass in?" he asked.

"Uh-huh."

"What I owe you?"

Daniel stood up and flapped the box shut. "Nothing. I'll get it out of the landlord."

"Shit, man, he ain't gonna pay for nothing. I busted it, I oughta pay for it."

"You busted it?"

"Yeah. Last night. Slammed the door too hard." He dug into his pocket. "Five bucks enough?"

"Too much. Window only cost two-fifty."

"Hell, man, you ought to get something for your time."

"Two-fifty's good enough."

Smith handed him the money. "I don't guess we met before," he said. "My name's Smith. A. L. Smith."

"Daniel Hews." They shook hands. "Thanks for owning up about the window."

"Well, I busted it."

The silence was deeper than if they had never talked at all.

Daniel opened his door. "Well, guess I'll get some sleep," he said.

"Yeah. That's a good idea. Night, Mr. Hews." A.L. waved his wide hand and then dropped it to the rickety banister. He heaved himself up the narrow stairwell, using the banister for support. The steps groaned and wheezed beneath his bulk.

He unlocked his door and clicked on the light as he pulled the silver construction worker's hat from his head and tossed it onto the broken-down couch. He was hungry.

Rubbing his big belly beneath the faded blue sweatshirt, A.L. opened the door of the low refrigerator and bent over to peer into it, trying to see in the dark because the fixture for the light inside had shorted out months ago and the landlord hadn't got around to fixing it. Just like the time the plaster had fallen from the ceiling in the bathroom from the years of being steamed, leaving the laths and chicken wire still exposed.

He stuck his wide hand inside the box, pulled out a package of hot dogs, and looked at them carefully, feeling slightly unsteady as he tried to decide whether he wanted hot dogs or not. He put them back and closed the door, then reopened it and took out a half-gallon container of milk. Walking into the living room, he sat down on the couch, drinking noisily, his mustache white from the milk.

He sat holding the container between his legs, looking at the paint-peeled wall across from him. The paint had been fresh last fall, but the winter with heat and then no heat had cracked it and now it was peeling from the cracked plaster beneath it. He would have liked some lamps around instead of the glaring naked bulb in the center of the ceiling, but none of the outlets worked any more and there was little hope of getting them fixed without rewiring the entire house.

He dropped his big head back against the top of the couch and closed his eyes, thinking about the time when he had been a fighter with a promising career, twenty years old and not lugging an ounce of fat around with him. Ten fights, all knock-outs, and he'd only been hit once. It wasn't a bad record, he decided, even if most of the guys had been punch-drunk stumble-bums on their way down. He no longer felt the anger he had then at having to give it all up, or rather having it taken away from him. He was just as well out of the ring, and he would never have gotten his job as foreman on the construction crew at the bridge but for his time in the ring and his size. Learning to read blueprints with only eight years of school behind him had been the toughest part. But after six years he knew his job and he earned good money, and it wasn't hard work like his father had had on the fishing boats, which killed him.

Maybe it was like some cats said, that things worked out for the best, and yet maybe, just maybe he could have been a champ. In a way it was his own fault, because if he hadn't blown his cool in the bar when that little white cat started mouthing off, he would still be fighting. What he hated most was the memory of those three years in Sing-Sing and that white mother-fucking judge who had sent him up.

He'd showed them, though. His wide mouth spread into a grin, yeah, he'd showed them. He could still tear a little ass on his own and do it by their rules. And it was always a challenge because every time they hired a new bunch there was always one who wasn't going to take orders from him and he got to pound his head once or twice before the cat gave in and either left or went to work.

He lifted the container of milk and guzzled, finally emptying the red and blue carton. This place wasn't fit for even the rats that lived in it, or the cockroaches either. Even when he tried to fix it up, the attempts ended in failure. Maybe he'd move, find a place he could fix up, one that would stay fixed. He had enough money, maybe even enough to buy a place himself and rent apartments, good apartments, and there'd be no fucking around about busting the place up, because he'd come down on them and they would know it.

He stood looking out the front window at the house across the street. The whole damn neighborhood was falling down. As he stared through the dirty panes of glass something caught his eye. He thought it was in one of the upstairs windows, but now that he looked hard there was nothing but the blankness of a ruined house. He wished they'd hurry up and tear it down. At least then the junkies would have to look for some place else to hole up.

He shut off the lights and wandered into the bedroom. As he drifted slowly toward sleep he was still thinking about the possibility of becoming a landlord. "You're going soft in the head," he mumbled to himself as he rolled over on his side.

5

In the morning, before it was light, Billy finished the last of the food he had bought with the money from the grocery store and walked out of the tunnel into the misty dawn which even the car headlights seemed unable to penetrate. He walked down the tracks and up the concrete walkway and then back around the block to the bridge below the dam. The streets were deserted except for a scattering of trucks and early buses. He stood on the bridge looking down into the dirty water boiling along toward where the construction crews were starting to work, only half visible in the mist hanging over the river. He liked the way their shouts carried up out of the fog and the machinery sounded heavy and throaty as if it were having trouble breathing in the cold gray mist.

The noise reminded him of the time he and his father had sat high up on the ridge in the government woods and watched the men working to put a road through. His father had cursed steadily as they waited for night and a chance to break up the big machines. That road had meant an end to their poaching lumber out of the forest.

Behind him now the sun had broken over the horizon like a bowl of golden warmth tipped and suddenly runneling through the deserted city streets.

As the traffic grew steadily thicker he turned away from the river, leaning against the railing of the bridge to watch the people walking by. They were dressed in clothes that people back home only wore to church or when they traveled to Atlanta. He started walking with the people, moving at their pace, passing store windows filled with fancy clothes as the crowd carried him into the center of the business district. He stopped to look at the clothes, reading the price tags and wondering why any man would pay a hundred dollars for clothes which had neither warmth nor strength. The shoes were all low-cut and useless. They were pretty to look at, like women's shoes, but how could a man keep his feet dry in them or keep from twisting an ankle? Yet everywhere he looked on the street the men wore the same sort of shoes, and they cost thirty dollars. His new boots had only cost fifteen.

Along the street near the alley entrance to the Midtown Mall, a boy was selling flowers in bright bunches. Billy watched as the men stopped to buy them, or just a single one for their coats. He had never seen men wearing flowers before, except once at a wedding.

He moved on, wrapped in another group of people, and now he listened to two large women in front of him, talking as they wobbled along on high heels.

"It's hard to believe, Grace," one of them said. Even her legs were fat, and her weight made them bow at the ankles as she walked, giving her a peculiar side-to-side wobble. It was the way you walked, Billy decided, after you had stepped in dog shit.

" . . . That poor boy, all alone in the grocery store. . . . "

Their voices were high and tight with excitement, and Billy liked the sound of them. He followed along for several blocks, listening. Once the fat one turned and looked over her shoulder, but her eyes focused beyond Billy as if he were not there.

At the next corner the two women stepped into the street and started running across. Billy froze, remembering what his father had told him about running when other people were walking, how it attracted attention. Still, he did not understand why they had suddenly run from him, and he watched as they reached the other side, his body tense, ready to run himself if they turned and looked back at him. They did not turn, but continued on into the store, adjusting their hats as they attacked the revolving doors. It was not until he saw the small sign across the street that he understood. As he waited the sign changed to "walk" and he obeyed, walking slowly across the street.

Now upwind of the people in front of him, he was aware of a change. At first they merely seemed uneasy, as if a rainstorm were coming on. The men hunched their shoulders inside their lightweight coats and some, especially the women, sniffed the air as they turned.

He tried moving with several groups before he realized that they were reacting to him, that he smelled from not having had a bath in nearly a month. He spent the rest of the morning by himself.

By noon he was very hungry and the streets were thick with the smell of cooking food. He headed back to the tunnel, where he crawled in under the crates. No matter how hungry he was, he would have to stay here until dark. There were just too many people around and he didn't know enough about this place yet.

He curled himself into his blanket and fell asleep. It was well after dark when he opened the blanket and rolled out. Already the place was different. The pattern of sounds outside had changed again and he left quickly, driven by his hunger. He climbed quickly out of the canyon formed by the concrete bulkheads. It was almost as deserted as it had been the first night. He thought about going to that store again, but there was sure to be some law there now.

He walked with his hands in the side pockets of his jacket so he could hold himself more tightly against the raw damp of spring. As he walked along, Billy reminded himself to lay in some extra food this time. It was not good to be too hungry. You made mistakes that way.

A police cruiser rolled slowly by and he kept his pace exactly the same, not looking directly at the car, but checking it out of the corners of his eyes. They had not even looked and he began to feel more secure. The quicker he learned, the safer he would be.

He was a block from the river when he turned onto a wide street. It was much brighter here, with the windows in the stores all lit up, and as he walked along he began picking up the smell of food again. He turned at the first street that ran back toward the river. It was a bright street too, but not as bright as the one he had turned from. Down across the dark reach of the bridge he could see a small group of stores. Across from them it was dark, and he guessed that must be where he had watched the men working. Walking down that way, he moved in closer to the buildings, trying to cut down his silhouette. He was moving quietly and easily, trying not to rush. There was only very light traffic, and several of the stores were completely dark except for a lone light back inside.

Had he been walking fast he would not have spotted the man in time, squatting in the doorway of a shoe store, working on something near the ground.

Billy never stopped walking, just came in on the man from the back and slightly to one side, his last four steps covering the distance between them with the speed of a stalking cat. He slipped his knife around front and drew it quickly, catching the man as he fell backward and sitting him down in the darkened doorway.

He wiped off his knife on the man's narrow tie and pulled out his shirttail to clean the blood from the hilt of the knife. It took him several minutes to find the man's wallet, because it was not in the back pants pocket where most men carried them, but inside his coat. Billy counted twenty-seven dollars.

When he stepped from the doorway a big, dark man with a package under his arm was turning the corner out of sight two blocks down. Billy knew from the way he was walking that he had not seen and that he was drunk.

He walked out to the grocery store and bought some food and returned to the tunnel. Before going to sleep he tucked half of the money and the rest of his food behind a loose stone in the wall where the mortar had cracked away. He blocked the cracks with small stones from the floor of the tunnel and then, curling himself into a ball, slept without stirring, not even to switch away the cockroach that dashed across his forehead, or to chase the rats that swarmed around him, drawn by the smell of the food but held off by Billy's scent, sitting up on their hind legs and twitching their noses against the dark, moist air.

6

DANIEL HEWS walked out through the gate, his black aluminum lunch pail swinging from his hand in rhythm to his bowlegged stride. He turned at the first corner and walked up to the next street where he picked up the bus that carried him to work.

The morning was unusually clear and dry, with the sun still at a sunrise angle. He was comfortable in his light jacket as he waited alone at the bus stop, watching an occasional car until it disappeared around the corner up by the Circle Market. One of the red trucks from the newspaper pulled up and the man climbed out, trotting with an armload of papers which he tossed into the red dispensing machine.

He jogged back to his truck, and Daniel walked over to look into the glass and metal stand. He had never seen such a big headline, just three words running all the way across the paper.

STABBER STRIKES AGAIN

Police said today that a Harvard Street man found stabbed to death early this morning in front of his Main Street store was probably slain by the same killer who just three nights ago murdered an all-night grocery clerk.

The stabber's second victim was Samuel A. Stein, 53, of 620 Harvard St., the owner of Stein's Shoe Store on Main Street East. His empty wallet was found next to his body where it was apparently dropped by the killer, police said.

Daniel couldn't see the next line because of the fold in the paper and he had only the two quarters to get him to work and home. He hunkered down close to the sidewalk but he still couldn't make them out.

He suddenly remembered that usually people left papers on the bus, and he walked to the curb and looked off down the empty street. He could not see the bus. He walked out into the middle of the street, but the road curved away and he could only see a block behind. "Goddamn bus," he mumbled as he walked back onto the curb and over to the newspaper box, staring through the glass window at the paper. The metal was thin, light gauge. Maybe he could pop it open and grab a paper. He looked around slowly. The street was deserted. He set his lunch pail on the pavement next to his oil-stained work boot, started to reach for the box, and then stopped. He turned slowly, looking carefully at the windows of the houses across the street and then at those above his head. No one watching. Again he reached toward the red vending machine, and then suddenly he saw himself breaking open the box to steal a newspaper and he yanked his hand away as if the box were as hot as its brilliant red color. He picked up his lunch pail and walked over to wait for the bus, shaking his head as he looked down at the trash packed in the gutter. "What for?" he said aloud. "To read about some stupid murder?" It was goddamn crazy.

The doors opened with a sharp hiss and Daniel climbed quickly aboard, standing with his legs spread against the forward surge of the bus as he fished for the quarter in the tight pockets of his jeans. He dropped it into the glass box and turned toward the back of the bus, looking for a paper. He couldn't see one anywhere. The bus was empty and even the floors were clean.

He sat down in the front facing the side wall behind the driver. One of the guys at work was sure to have a paper anyway, which meant he'd only have to wait maybe twenty minutes. He crossed his feet at the ankles, the outside edges of his boots flattened against the floor as he looked down at the worn rubber matting surrounding the driver. There was a newspaper next to the driver's lunch pail.

Daniel leaned forward. "You got this morning's paper?"

The driver looked at him out of the corner of his eye. "They only cost a dime," he said.

"I only got the quarter I gave you to carry me to work and one more to get home."

The driver didn't turn, but reached down and grabbed the paper, crossing hands to keep one on the wheel while he reached out with the other to hand the paper to Daniel. "Make sure I get it back," he said.

"Uh-huh, thanks."

He reread he first part of the story down to the fold and then picked up as he flipped the paper over.

Stein, according to police, often worked late, going over his accounts and books.

His body was found by Officer Charles Cirullo as he was checking doors along his beat just after 2 A.M.

Police still have no clues to the identity of the killer, though they said last night it was probably the same man who killed the grocery clerk. According to Detective Capt. James Ansella, the killer wipes his knife or razor clean on the shirt or tie of his victim and he only takes cash, leaving the change behind.

"We're working around the clock," Ansella said this morning, "but this is the hardest kind of murder to solve. We don't have a lot to go on."

Daniel folded the paper and handed it back to the driver. "Thanks," he said. "I wanted to read about that killer." He scratched at the tangle of black hair that cascaded from his ears, poking first at the right and then the left. "Think they'll catch him?"

"Sure," the driver said back over his shoulder, not taking his eyes off the road. "I'm glad I ain't got a night run though. You never know about those nuts. But this ain't New York City, you know. They'll catch him. Not enough places to hide in a city this size. Now you take that strangler they had in Boston. Pretty hard to find in a city that big. But here, what've we got? Three hundred thousand people? Hell, buddy, there ain't no way he can stay loose for long."

"You think that's what it is? Some insane person?"

"Sure, buddy. Who else? Even niggers don't kill people the way this guy does."

"Sure is strange, ain't it?"

"My wife was telling me this morning that it ain't safe no more, you know? She says I ought to get a gun or something to protect us, and I told her I had enough of guns in the war. But you know how women are. She'll keep nagging and nagging until I get a gun, then first thing you know the cops'll catch the killer and two weeks later she'll want to know how come I keep a gun around. I tell you, buddy, I don't know what we're coming to, you know what I mean?"

"Sure do," Daniel said.

The bus began to slow and Daniel, already leaning forward, turned his head to look out the wide front window. He could see a small, blond-haired kid waiting at the bus stop, and instantly his breath caught in his throat and his heart picked up a couple of beats. As the bus drew to a stop and the doors hissed open, his heart began to level off again. For a second, just as he first looked up, he had thought it was his cousin. He sat back in the seat, watching the kid drop his coin into the box and walk by him toward the back of the bus. Why would he suddenly think of Billy? He was way down Georgia, and . . . and it came crashing in on him like a stone through a nighttime window. How could he have missed it? Billy Oakes. It had to be! Even now after six years he couldn't really forget that afternoon up by the tall loblolly pines, not the blood or Billy's twisted smile or the sunlight in bright patches on the needle-soft ground. God, how he had wanted to run! But he had just stood there, rooted as solid as the big pine he had leaned against to keep from falling down. Even later he had been afraid to tell anyone what had happened, knowing Billy would come after him. The Oakeses always did. It wasn't safe even when they were in prison, because you couldn't depend on them not getting out. Those killings in the paper had all the earmarks of an Oakes. He knew better than anybody, because the one image he retained whole from that afternoon in the pines was Billy carefully wiping off his knife with Charlie Clay's shirt. But Billy had to be down Georgia; he wouldn't leave the mountains. He was afraid even when they went down to the general store.

But maybe Billy thought Daniel would tell someone and had come looking for him. He was crazy enough to try.

Each stop now they picked up four and five people until the bus was so crowded that people were standing, holding onto the metal bar overhead and the handles on the backs of the seats. Daniel chuckled to himself. He was getting to be a nervous wreck. He was worried about some kid stealing his job, and if that wasn't enough he had to go making up things because of the way he felt about his cousin. He decided to talk to his foreman first thing about those classes.

7

BILLY WASN'T SURE at first whether the two men were talking about it or not, but he followed along behind them anyway. The sounds of their voices were as much alike as their clothes, and except for the funny little suitcases they were carrying they could have been going to church.

They walked in step. Crossing curbs, if one or the other got out of rhythm he would skip on the off-beat to bring himself back to the cadence. Billy found it hard to separate the two men.

"Did you see the paper this morning?" the one on the right asked.

The response and the next few words they exchanged were lost in the roar of an accelerating bus. At least the two men were comfortable to follow because their pace was very even.

"They got any suspects?" They were jammed together at a street corner, waiting for the light.

"No."

"You think it's one of those gangland things?"

"In *Lakeport?* I think it's some crazy nigger."

"Hey, watch it, will you?" He looked quickly around, his gaze sweeping past Billy.

The light changed, and as they started across several people came between Billy and the two men. The last thing he heard one of them say was, "You've spent too much time in Chicago."

On the other side of the street Billy slowed his pace, drifting in close to the storefronts where people didn't notice if you walked slower. In the glass he could see the people walking by.

The morning was cushioned in a warm haze and if the breeze died it would get very hot. He swung out away from the windows and walked in the stream of people again, trying to keep enough distance to prevent them from picking up his odor. The breeze was no help because it was unsteady and it changed direction at every corner. Not trusting the breeze, he had to hang back so far it was impossible to hear what people were saying.

Finally he gave up rather than risk getting close enough to hear over the deep hiss of the traffic. And he was afraid too they would suddenly turn and know that he was listening.

For a while he sat on one of the benches on Broad Street watching the people walk by. There were two smelly old men either side of him who hadn't shaved in days. They were both sleeping. It was comfortable sitting in the sun that filtered through the dusty air, and it was almost noon when he decided to move again, to walk up to the clock. It had big tubes that were mounted on arms extended out like the spokes of a wagon wheel. At noon those tubes opened up, and there were dolls inside that danced and whirled. He liked the gay music.

As he stood watching the dolls in their jerky dance, Billy picked up a quick movement out of the corner of his eye and turned slightly to watch a tall, wide-shouldered nigger weaving through the crowd, walking fast and light. He had a heavy paunch hanging out over his belt, bulging his faded blue shirt, but he was young and moved easily, sliding his bulk in and around the standing people. At the far end of the mall he pushed into a bank. When he came back out, he was walking slowly, counting a fistful of money. As he finished he slowly rolled the bills into a tight coil and wound an elastic band around it, flipping it once in the air and finally stuffing it into the pocket of his work pants. His boots were gray, with dried mud covering the bottom of the shoes and part of the sides. Now he walked leisurely, both hands slung in the slash pockets of his green jacket. His shiny silver metal hat was cocked to one side.

He disappeared in the crowd and Billy saw the hat flash once at the doors. He was sure it was the man he had seen going into Daniel's house.

When the clock finished its performance Billy followed after the big man. He stopped when he came to the street, looking both ways, but he could not see him.

He stood at the corner watching the people and the traffic and looking at the tall buildings on both sides of the street. The restlessness was barking inside him like a dog on a short chain. He waited at the corner, not sure which way to go, until finally the restlessness drove him on in a fast-paced rolling sort of walk that carried him onto East Avenue and on down past the shops filled with clothing.

He walked a block and turned into an alley, crossing back out to Main Street only to turn again at the next corner. He spent the rest of the day walking through the area, turning as the whim hit him, never stopping, just picking random streets. By the time it was dark he was tired and hungry, and he headed back toward the tunnel.

He sat on one of the crates eating slowly, thinking about that nigger with the thick roll of money. He had been thinking about him off and on all day, trying to figure out how much was in that roll. As he had done before, he tried to push the thought away. The man was too big and too strong. He looked as if he had done a lot of fighting. With a man that size he would have to be perfect with his knife. There were easier targets.

When he finished eating, he rolled himself into his blanket. He was drowsy, but he did not sleep at first; instead he twisted and tossed on the straw and paper bed. Finally, thinking about Georgia and the Smokies, he began to relax. He had been happy there in the hills with no one to get in his way. Maybe he would go back soon. He drifted into sleep.

It was still dark when a train panting at the entrance to the tunnel woke him. He crouched down behind the crates, hiding from its glaring white eye, not even breathing until it had passed him. The heavy diesel fumes settling to the floor of the tunnel drove him out into the air.

He walked again, at first aimlessly and then back toward East Avenue and the big houses he had passed during the day. There were no people on the sidewalks now, and the cars and trucks which had cluttered the street were gone.

The sky was lighter in the east and a small breeze kicked some dust out of the gutter, swirling it skyward with a few tiny scraps of paper. The sun was still lurking well below the horizon, and the air seemed heavy and dense once the breeze had passed.

The lights on the single car that passed him barely penetrated the gloom.

In a garden behind one of the houses, Billy found a bird bath. He stripped to the waist and took a bar of soap from his pocket. In the half-light he splashed himself with the cold water, soaped down, and then rinsed himself by scooping handfuls of water from the bath. The long streams of water dampened the beltline of his pants, and he took them off and continued washing, periodically shaking his naked body like a wet dog.

The lights were on upstairs in the house and downstairs in the back wing. He picked up his clothes and walked behind the garage where, screened by a clump of bushes, he dressed slowly, enjoying the cool air on his body.

Before putting on his shirt he pulled out the knife and tested the edge against his thumb nail. It was not as sharp as he liked it, but it would do. He slipped it back into the sheath and put his shirt on.

He climbed in through the back window of the garage and into the back seat of the big Cadillac limousine, crouching low behind the driver's seat, waiting now almost without breathing.

The chauffeur was the first to come out to the garage, whistling at the morning as he opened the big bay door and slipped into the driver's seat. Billy slit his throat with a sharp, snapping flick of his wrist. The only sound was the knife at work and a gasping chortle.

Billy wiped his knife carefully on the man's shirttails and slid the body under the big, black car. He closed the big bay door, walked over and waited by the side door, picking that one purely by instinct, not thinking about it, not trying to guess which door the man would use. He froze into position inside, leaning like a praying mantis, pitched slightly forward, the knife ready.

John Conant Reed came looking for his chauffeur, stamping across the lawn, angry at being late for the office.

"Charles!" he shouted. "Charles! Where in hell are you!"

He ignored what should have been a warning when Charles did not answer, and came storming into the garage through the side door. Billy slapped one hand over Reed's mouth and pulled him backward onto the blade.

After wiping off the knife, he went through their pockets. The chauffeur had ten dollars, Reed forty-six. Billy left the garage the way he had entered, through the rear window. Outside, he stayed with the heavily budded hedges, crossing into the back yard of the neighboring house. When he reached the sidewalk he stood up and walked off down the street, without hurrying or looking back.

8

THE WEATHER was unusually warm for May, and as Daniel walked down Clarissa Street toward the gray cyclone fence which separated his house from the others, he thought about the Memorial Day weekend and the picnic he and Sarah had been planning since the ground had first thawed in the spring. It was nearly an hour's drive to the state park, and he didn't know whether the old wreck of a Nash would make it both ways. The first problem was whether he could even get it started.

But right now, with the warm weather coming on and things beginning to work out, it didn't really matter. By next year this time they'd be a lot better off and maybe they could even afford a better car.

The warm air had drawn the kids out onto the street again, and their shouting and running surrounded him, wrapping his excitement in an even brighter package. Today he loved everybody, and he smiled at the kids as he sidestepped their skip-rope game so they wouldn't have to stop.

He still could not quite believe he was so smart, but he had the proof. He had got the best marks in the class on their first test, and the teacher had told him afterward that if he continued to do so well he would qualify for a raise and a chance to take a special class in math and blueprint reading. He guessed he worked for the best company there was.

It still surprised him that so many Negroes couldn't read. He didn't understand how even though most of them had gone to school, they hadn't learned to read. Maybe what the preacher said back home was right. Maybe they weren't as smart as white people. He'd never seen enough of them to know. They mostly didn't live in the mountains.

He hesitated at the gate, looking up at the gray ruin of the house. For the first time it didn't look so bad. One of the guys in the shop had just come up from North Carolina, and he had to sleep in his car. Every time he went looking for a room in a decent place they slammed the door in his face. He figured it was his accent, and Daniel had decided right then, he was going to learn to talk the way people up here did. This was his home now. The old things were behind him. They belonged to another time and place, and they were useless up here.

He whistled his way up the walk and he was still whistling when he opened the door and came face-to-face with a tall colored girl. In the light from the door window he could tell she was young, but her skin was greasy looking.

"Does A.L. Smith still live here?"

"Uh-huh, upstairs," Daniel said. Her clothes were cheap, her hair had been straightened and dyed red, and her perfume filled the entire hall, thick and heavy, syrupy as molasses on a hot day.

"You know what time he comes in?"

"No. You want me to give him a message?"

She looked down at the floor, as if unable to figure out why a hillbilly was being so nice. "Naw," she said, "that's all right. I come back later." She stepped back so he could open the door and then walked on out.

Daniel watched her twitching her behind down the path to the gate and suddenly he was angry with himself for having asked about the message. Hell, she wasn't nothing but a two-bit whore. He watched her work the gate latch. But what the hell, Smith seemed like a nice enough guy and he had to get his ass somewhere. Daniel opened the door and walked on through the living room toward the kitchen.

"Hello, honey," Sarah said as he set his empty lunch pail on the wobbly-legged table, then crossed and kissed her on the back of her neck. She tasted sweet and fresh, and the warm familiarity made him forget the girl in the hall.

"Hi," he said as he kissed her again behind her right ear.

"You watch it now, Daniel," she laughed, the delight in her voice as fresh as her smell.

He opened the refrigerator and took out a beer, then had to rummage around in the drawer for the opener. She turned away from the stove as he sat at the table. "Want a beer?" he asked.

"No. I'm getting too fat," she said.

He just smiled and Sarah, knowing what the smile meant, sat down quickly at the table. "You sure are in a funny mood today."

"Well, it's a good day. I found out that I'm at the top of the class, and the guy who runs it told me that if I stayed up over an eighty-five average I was sure to get a big raise and a chance to take the class in math and blueprint reading." He tipped up his beer bottle, watching her as he drank.

"Oh, Daniel! I can't believe it! Really?"

"Uh-huh."

She held her face in both hands, shaking her head from side to side. "Oh, Daniel, I just can't believe it!"

"I figure with the raise and not having to use the bonus to pay for doctor bills next year, we ought to be able to move out of here."

She reached across the table and took his right hand between both of hers, holding it to her neck. "That's the best news I've heard since you told me we were leaving Georgia."

“Where are the kids?” he asked.

“Out back playing. They’ll be out another half-hour at least.”

“C’mon,” he said as he stood and took her hand.

She followed behind him up the stairs and into the bedroom. She liked it this way, when his need was strong and there was an urgency like the first time, up behind the spring.

Afterward as they both lay naked on top of the bed, smoking in the darkened room, she remembered the woman who had come that afternoon.

“That woman come again today,” she said.

“Which woman?”

“The one I told you about. Mrs. Clarke. She brought me some more books and some for you too.”

“How much does she charge?”

“Nothing.”

“It really is free, huh?”

“Yes. She works for the county. She has something to do with some kind of a program for making people . . .”

“Literate?”

“Uh-huh, I think that’s the word she used. I never heard it before.” She rested, her head propped on one arm so she could see his strong nose and chin as he lay on his back, silhouetted against the light from the open door.

“Hard to believe it’s all for free, ain’t it?”

“She’s real nice. And she’s gonna come once a—” A door banged downstairs and Sarah jumped off the bed and began dressing quickly. She paused at the door and looked back at Daniel, lying with his hands folded behind his head, the big muscles in his arms drawn tight. He hadn’t been as good since Ginger had been born.

Daniel didn’t get to the newspaper until after dinner, and it wasn’t until he had settled into the chair with Duke and Ginger playing around his feet that he saw the big headline on page one.

INDUSTRIALIST, CHAUFFEUR MURDERED

John Conant Reed, 55, of 420 East Ave., and his chauffeur, Charles Ackly, 38, of the same address, were found stabbed to death just after dawn this morning, police said.

Reed, vice-president for land acquisition for Kapco, Inc., was found just inside the door of his garage by his cook, Margret Himple. Ackly's body was found by police next to the Reed limousine.

All the characteristics of the double murder were the same as the two previous stabbings just over two weeks ago, according to police. The shirttails of both men had been pulled out by the killer to wipe the blood from his knife or razor.

The killer, according to Detective Capt. James Ansella, entered the garage through a rear window and waited in the back seat of the car for Ackly.

He then stationed himself inside the side door, waiting for Reed.

The pockets of both men had been turned inside out, and only the bills were taken.

Ansella said that tracks outside the rear window indicated the killer left the same way he entered. He said the tracks indicated the man is medium height and weight, probably around five-seven and 150 pounds.

Ansella asked for the public's help. Anyone having noticed a man of that size in the area this morning is requested to come to police headquarters and ask for Capt. Ansella.

The two murders this morning bring to four the total number of similar killings in just over two weeks.

Police Chief Lemuel Barton, contacted at headquarters today, termed the killings the work of an obvious psychopath and warned residents not to go out alone at night and not to open their door to strangers either night or day.

Daniel dropped the paper into his lap, aware that he had read right through the story without hesitating once. He went back and reread the details of the killings, studying. Wiping off the knife sounded right, but it wasn't like Billy to leave tracks anywhere, though he guessed from the story that the tracks hadn't told much.

"C'm'on you two," Sarah said as she came in from the kitchen. "Time for bed. Say goodnight to Daddy."

They both scrambled up onto his lap to be kissed and then, still high from playing, giggled their way up the stairs with Sarah herding them from behind.

Daniel got up out of the chair and began looking for a piece of paper and a pencil. When he found them, he had to hunt for an envelope, finally finding one in the back of a bureau drawer. He even managed to find a stamp.

He sat hulked over the metal-topped kitchen table, slowly working out the words on the piece of lined paper. The entire letter to Aunt May contained only three sentences: "Where is Billy? I think he is here in Lakeport. Do you know?" He signed it Daniel Hews in big, printed letters.

He printed her address on the envelope, sealed it, and stuck the stamp in the upper right corner. He slid the letter into his pocket and walked into the living room just as Sarah was coming back downstairs. He took his jacket out of the narrow closet.

"Where are you going?"

"Just for a walk. It's nice out."

She looked at him carefully, trying to read what he wasn't telling her, but his expression was set.

"Don't be gone too long," she said as he opened the door.

Outside the night was sharp, the air filled with the edges of frost they would not see again until late October. He pulled the collar of his jacket up around the back of his neck and stuffed his hands in the pockets as he kicked the gate shut behind him. The mailbox was up where he waited for the bus, and he walked along quickly, enjoying the smell of the dusty dampness.

He hoped Aunt May would answer right off. He had to know, even though he had not figured out what he was going to do if Billy was in town. He knew his cousin well enough to know he'd be somewhere watching, staying back out of sight, waiting for his chance.

Several cars passed as he walked the broken sidewalk past the black-faced houses, skirting piles of trash and broken glass on the rotted cement surface. When he stopped to wait for a car before crossing a side street, he felt a soft tickle at the back of his neck. Unconsciously he rubbed it away. The second time he felt it, he knew he was being followed. He turned suddenly into the dark behind him, staring hard, but he couldn't see anything. He held his breath, listening for any slight sound, but whoever it was now stood frozen into the silent dark. When Daniel started across the street, he heard him move. It was a tiny sound, not the kind most people who live in the city would be aware of, almost as easy as a puff of wind settling into a pine tree, but Daniel heard it as clearly as if it had been a pistol shot. He had given himself away by turning, and whoever was following could not be taken by surprise.

He stopped in front of the mailbox, taking his time so he could look back down the side street as he slipped the letter from his pocket and into the box, letting the flap clang shut. He walked slowly back down the side street, keeping to the outside edge of the pavement where it would give him an extra step if his follower were waiting. Once on Clarissa Street, he stopped and lit a cigarette, holding his breath and sucking the flame from the hole in his cupped hands. He heard nothing and the tickle was gone from the back of his neck. Maybe he had been imagining things.

When he turned and started back toward the house he felt it almost immediately. Someone, somewhere was following him, staying well back, but he could feel the eyes hunting him from the cover of the darkness. He did not turn now or increase his pace, but fought inside to hold it steady even as the urge to run grew so fast that he knew his hands were shaking. He stuffed them into his pockets. He could see the gate up ahead and it looked a thousand miles away, and though he steadily closed the distance, it seemed to get further away until suddenly he had his hand on the latch. He opened the front door quietly and stood inside for several minutes, looking back out into the street, searching for a tiny difference from the way it usually looked, but he could see nothing out of order. Yet even inside he could feel those eyes peering at the door. He scanned the face of the house across the street, satisfying himself that it looked the same as always. Shit, he mumbled to himself. Probably some damn junkie all doped up and staggering around in the dark back up some alley where he couldn't be seen.

"Have a nice walk?" Sarah was sitting watching their old wreck of a television.

"Uh-huh." He took off his jacket. "Nice night." He hung up the jacket and flopped into his big, shabby chair, staring at the flickering blue picture. It had to be Billy. Only his cousin could follow him that way, so well, so easily. He wondered if anyone else in the house could have seen him. Maybe Smith upstairs. He doubted it. Who would notice Billy Oakes, even if they bumped into him on the street? He wasn't the kind of man you saw.

9

A.L. WATCHED the new kid coming up on the platform that dangled on thick cables at the end of the crane. He was the last one out of the pit. It had been a cold motherfucker down there in the morning. Only come summer would it be better and then it would be almost a relief to work in the cool damp of the coffer dams.

But this time of year A.L. got out of the pit every time there was a break. He would find the sunniest spot he could and stretch out, trying to absorb enough heat to last the afternoon. Today the sun was bright and warm, and it made him feel cat-lazy as he sat down on a nail keg in front of the timekeeper's shack. He decided to have more coffee before opening the grinder he had bought at the kosher deli on Main Street.

He took off his polished steel hat and set it upside down on the ground next to him. He was so sleepy from the sun that he wasn't sure he would get through his lunch. But his stomach was empty and the hot coffee was reviving him, beating back the chill that had got into him from working below the level of the river.

As he peeled back the paper on the big grinder he saw the new kid walking toward him, weaving his way around the piles of equipment and rubble on the site. He was a big, strong kid and he seemed happy about having a job. He'd quit high school only two weeks ago.

"Okay if I sit down, Mr. Smith?"

"Go ahead."

He sat down on a piece of scrap pipe and opened his lunch pail. "They tell me you used to be a fighter," he said.

A.L. poured another cup of coffee from his big thermos. "That's right."

"What was your record?"

"Ten and 0."

"How many knockouts?"

"All knockouts." He took a swallow of coffee and set the cup on the ground so he could work on the grinder. He knew what was coming.

"How come you quit?"

"Sing-Sing."

"What'd they bust you for?"

"I got into a pushing contest with a white cat and somebody called the cops. When it came to court the only witnesses turned out to be white. Not even my manager showed up. The guy said I hit him and the judge said three years."

The kid was quiet, munching a fat peanut butter and jelly sandwich, mostly jelly. "That wouldn't happen now," he said.

"What makes you think it wouldn't?"

"We got organizations keep those white motherfuckers in line."

A.L. watched him carefully as he finished off his grinder and picked up the cup of coffee, wondering how long it would take the kid to get around to it. He couldn't count the number of them that had walked into the gym back in Harlem. They all wanted to be fighters, but after looking around the gym at some of the punchy ex-fighters, they would change their minds.

"You want to be a fighter?" A.L. asked.

The kid looked at him, his eyes boring in. "Yeah, well I thought about it, you know. I'd like to learn to handle myself like you with that polak this morning."

"It ain't hard to learn."

"You teach me?"

"Maybe."

"That sure was something, all right. I think your left hand is fast as Clay's."

A.L. finished his coffee and poured another cup. "That's because you ain't seen Clay. Guys like that, Clay, Frazier, Marciano, Louis." He shook his head. "I tell you, maybe I was lucky to get busted by the law instead of getting busted by somebody like that. One time I went four rounds with one of Marciano's old sparring partners. The only reason I come out on top was that I was young and tough enough to take the best punch he had and come back. I got lucky in the fourth round and caught him with a left hook."

The kid was working on his second sandwich.

"What you want to fight for?" A.L. asked. "Whose head you got in mind you want to bust?"

"Nobody."

"Yeah, nobody. Like the principal of that high school you quit from?"

The kid looked up quickly.

"I mean, I ain't gonna teach you to fight so you can go around beating up on old men."

"He's not old. And anyway, he's white."

A.L. sighed. Obviously, this kid needed more in the way of education than just showing him how to throw a punch. He finished his coffee and tossed the sludge in the bottom of the cup away from them. "You see that bar down there?"

"Yeah."

"You meet me over there after quitting time, and we'll talk some more. Okay?"

The kid looked happy. "Yeah, okay." He got up and walked off toward the sanitation control shed. A.L. picked up his helmet and put it in place over his eyes as he leaned back against the wall of the shack. There was time for just a short nap before the whistle blew.

Usually he dropped off immediately, but talking to the kid had stirred up a lot of memories he'd just as soon forget. He wondered if the kid had a family, or just a mother. Probably just a mother and a mess of brothers and sisters, all of them crammed into a worse shit-hole than the one he lived in.

One of the things he'd learned from being in the ring and then in prison was that you had to make it yourself. There wasn't anyone about to help. Like his dream of someday owning his own apartment houses—the only way that was going to happen was if he went out and did it on his own. He had some money saved up and he'd have more by the end of the summer. All it took after that was some brains and a lot of hard work. The way he had it planned, he could buy in September and then he could get the place in shape over the winter when things were slow.

The first thing he would have to get done was the plumbing and wiring. There were a couple of guys he knew that would work for him and wouldn't be on his back all the time about money. The rest of the work, the carpentry, he could do himself.

The thought of having his own place was as exciting as the dreams he had had of being the champ. Maybe they were even more exciting. After all, this dream had a chance of coming true. Besides that, he didn't have all those people hanging around, gambler dudes and pimps, all trying to suck money out of him.

The shrill, short squawk of the whistle ended A.L.'s dreaming for a while, and he tipped his hat back into place and sat up. Off to his right, on the bridge, he could see a lone spectator.

Usually there was more than one, especially when the weather was so warm. For a second he stared up at the short, blond kid looking down at the job, his blond hair flopping in the wind. Probably can't find a job, A.L. decided. Got nothing better to do than stand up there watching other men work.

10

THE SECOND DAY after he killed the men in the garage, there was a change. At first he did not notice it except that walking at his usual pace he constantly fell behind and lost the ends of conversations. Even when he walked faster, it was hard to hear because they talked in harsh whispers through the noise from the traffic and the wind around the buildings.

At the corners where the crowd washed to a stop like water backing up at a dam, Billy heard one woman say the police weren't worth paying if they couldn't keep the streets safe at night.

Standing near a big gray building, he listened to two men talking: "I had to put up a whole set of floodlights around the house. Now my wife can't sleep unless I go buy a damned gun."

"Are they sure it's the same guy? What makes them think it isn't a gang thing?"

"The story I read said the chief thinks it's the work of some maniac like the Boston Strangler, except this guy robs his victims."

"Couldn't he just be a thief?"

"Come on, Harry, nobody kills for that little money."

"Don't they have any leads?"

"The paper said nobody has even seen him. They got some

footprints from the garden, but they're smooth and could have been made by anybody."

Billy looked down at his boots, suddenly forgetting whether he had cleaned the dirt from the soles. He had.

At the end of the mall he went into the drugstore and ordered a cup of coffee and a doughnut from one of the sky-blue ladies. The people there smelled of soap, some sweet like blooming flowers, or of sweat, new sweat and not like the bums on the benches.

He finished his coffee and walked back out into the mall. Even here the people were moving faster, and he walked toward the fountain near the end where some long-haired kids were sitting. For a while he sat on the edge of the pool under the fountain, just watching the people pause and scurry, thinking about home. The fishing in the mountain streams would just be getting good now, and the nights would come on cool but not cold any more.

He thought about Daniel's wife, remembering the time he had stood outside Sarah Ann's room in the dark watching her undress in front of her mirror. That had been before she married Daniel. His crotch felt tight as he remembered climbing in through the window afterward, moving without a sound on the balls of his feet until he stood at the foot of her bed. She had been naked in the moist heat, sleeping on her back, and when he woke her he had his big knife in one hand as he ran the other hand over her body. He would have gone further if her father had not come home then, causing him to run, diving out the window in a slow roll and then going off into the woods.

"Hey!"

He heard the voice, but did not connect it with himself.

"No sitting there, kid!"

Billy turned quickly, his head snapping around like a startled deer. The big cop was standing close, his hands on his hips. "Move along, kid."

Billy stood up and walked away toward the far door. His reflection in the window startled him. He had not realized how long his hair had grown. It hung clear over his ears, He pushed out through the door into the warm sunshine, just shuffling along, his hands stuffed into his pockets. He swung in behind a tall man in a dark suit. He had to pick up his pace to stay with him, though the man's height and his red hair flopping in the breeze made him easy to follow even in a thick crowd. Billy dodged easily in and out, keeping the man in sight until he disappeared into one of the buildings. When Billy walked by he could see him sitting at a big desk inside, lighting a cigarette as he studied some papers on his desk. He turned at the corner and drifted along the side street, then turned up a small alleyway.

He picked out a doorway deep enough to conceal him and then waited, huddled back into the shadow, even pulling his toes out of the diagonal slash of sunlight on the step. By dipping low he could look back down the alley over the top of a garbage can. He knew that he was invisible to anyone coming up into the sun, because of the brightness.

A fat man smoking a pipe walked out the back door of one of the buildings and came up the alley toward him. Billy slipped out his knife and crouched low, the muscles of his legs hard and ready to uncoil. The man moved closer, his big stomach bouncing unevenly but in cadence with his stride broken by the uneven cobbles. As he came abreast Billy tensed and then froze, holding himself back into the darkness as he heard another sound back near the entrance. He waited as the fat man passed him and then within less than a minute a thin woman walked by, balancing on her toes, trying to keep the long thin heels of her shoes from slipping into the crevices between the stones.

The man with the fur collar on his coat was not so lucky. As he passed, Billy snaked an arm out of the dark shadows, snapping it like a steel hook around the man's throat and following quickly with the knife, the way they slaughtered pigs back home.

Billy found the wallet with no trouble and pulled a wad of cash from it. He rolled it up and tucked it in his jacket pocket before wiping off his knife and walking off, leaving the man's legs sticking into the alley.

Within hours the streets were alive with people talking and looking back over their shoulders, searching into the faces of passing strangers, not knowing what they were looking for, but sure they would know when they saw it. Those who glanced at Billy looked away without hesitating, not even a flicker of suspicion in their eyes.

Billy listened. Now it was easy to catch people discussing the killer.

"Five men he's killed. Five men and the police haven't done one thing."

"It's not their fault, the radio said he's the hardest kind of killer to catch."

"Well, I told my husband he'd better buy a gun or we'll all end up murdered in our beds."

"The thing that gets me is, he hasn't killed a single woman. I thought these sadists or psychopaths or whatever they are usually went after women."

Billy decided to follow the one who was surprised the killer avoided women. Men with shoes like that were the best prey. It was the way he had hunted back in the mountains, following anything at all unless he cut the trail of something better.

"One of the guys in the office said he thought it was the work of a professional killer. One of those gang hoods."

"In Lakeport?"

"I don't know, the guy has got to be a pro of some kind to get away from the police so easily."

Billy liked that kind of remark. It was about him, about how well he had learned from his father. He would not make his father's mistake and kill someone he knew, even Daniel.

Past the river, down by an older building, red like the clay back home, a striped pole spinning around and around caught his attention. He stopped to look in the window behind the pole at the men sitting under sheets while men in white coats worked around their heads with scissors. He watched for several minutes before he realized it was a place where you got your hair cut, then walked in and sat down.

"Afternoon," one of the barbers said as he looked at Billy's long hair. He slung the sheet around him. "How long do you want it?"

"Huh?"

"How do you want it cut?"

Billy looked at the other men in the shop, checking their shoes first and then their hair. "Like that," he said, pointing to a man with expensive shoes.

"You mean short?" The barber smiled.

"Uh-huh."

11

SHE CAME OUT of the bank just as A.L. was crossing the street after work. He took off his hat and ran his hand over his close-cropped hair as he watched her move toward him, her hips swaying softly inside the gray tweed suit, which would have been better on a school teacher except that the hemline was well above her knees, showing her fine, thin legs. Looking up as she passed, he ran his finger around the leather head band inside the helmet. She was nearly six feet tall and her color was the rich brown he liked best, so different from his own, almost blue-black skin.

He dropped the hat back on his head and walked toward George's Saloon, watching her walk on up the street, swallowed by the cross-hatching people behind her. If she had noticed him she did not show it.

He pushed into the saloon, thick with people and smoke, and eased his way through, eyes down. She was the kind of woman who would never look once at him. He was better off with the whores and the occasional young girls he could knock off, girls who didn't give a shit what kind of a job he had, or that it was a dirty job. Getting tangled up with a woman like that would only be a heartbreak.

He dropped down onto the stool, pushing his tin hat up

away from his forehead. George always kept the same stool open for him, the last one near the kitchen, so he was away from the men he ordered around all day, and so they wouldn't feel restrained about their talk.

"Hello," George said, "you want steak tonight?" He wiped off the counter in front of A.L.

"Yeah, thanks, George," he said, "and maybe a beer, too."

George laughed.

He watched the stocky, solid Greek walk away toward the bar, which was nothing more than an extension of the counter. The saloon was only half full because of the weather. When it had been cold or raining off and on they all ended up at the saloon, nursing a shot and a beer, or if it happened to be payday they got drunk and it usually ended in his having to break up a fight. The worst one had been the day the pile-driver crew from downstate started mouthing off in the morning, almost before anybody had had time to get warm from the cold rain, and then kept it up all day.

Finally, after several false starts, a real fight had started. It couldn't have lasted more than a couple of minutes before A.L. broke it up, and nobody even got hurt. The bar was so narrow there just wasn't room to get a good shot, and after the first punch with everyone trying to get into the fight there was no room at all.

Now George threw the steak on the grill and sat down on the stool behind the counter directly across from A.L. There were only four men at the bar, all of them drinking quietly.

"This weather much better," George said.

"I was just thinking the same thing," A.L. said.

"No fights this way."

"Only when it rains."

"Good thing you here to stop that one. They bust up the whole place, otherwise." He chuckled in his characteristic sort of snort. "I never forget that look on the driver's face when you pick him off the floor."

A.L. grinned back. He had enjoyed his role as peace keeper at George's. Ever since that night, just his sitting here at the end of the bar was usually enough to keep anything from starting. The only trouble came when there was an out-of-town crew on the job.

"Who's that kid you talking to the other night?"

"He wants to be a fighter."

"You going to teach him?"

"Maybe. Depends on why he wants to learn. He's a good kid. Hard worker and he don't complain."

"He in your gang?"

"Yeah. Came on last week."

"Why you bother with him?"

"Don't know. I guess because I was once a big tough kid too. Maybe if somebody had bothered with me I would've made out better."

"What's wrong with what you got now?"

A.L. took a long swallow of beer and set the glass back down. "Nothing, I guess. I got some dough, a good job. Things ain't too bad." He thought of the houses. "I even got an idea to make some real dough."

"What you got?" George asked. His questions, because of his accent, sounded like challenges.

"What kind idea you got?" he repeated as he leaned both hands on the counter and cocked his head to one side.

"I got a roll in the bank, see, and I thought if I could get hold of a couple of houses in my part of town, I could fix them into nice places and rent out apartments."

"You ain't the first one had that idea," George said.

"I know, but my idea is to keep the places nice. What I'd do is come around once a week and make sure everything's okay. If it ain't I'll come down on them."

George went to the grill and turned the steak. He came back and stood looking intently at A.L. "It might work," he said. "The boys on the job, they plenty scared of you."

"It'd work," A.L. said as he emptied the glass of beer in front of him.

George picked up the glass and walked down toward the bank of taps. He stood straight with his chin pulled back as he poured the beer into the glass, cutting off the flow just before the narrow head reached the top. He did not waste a drop, nor did he make the head too thick.

A.L. sat staring at his big hands, his thick fingers slowly turning a packet of sugar over and over.

"Most of those houses are pretty old, huh?" George asked.

"I got my eye on a couple that ain't so bad. The bank says I gotta have a pretty big down payment though."

"How much?"

"The houses are both ten thousand, and the bank wants five grand on each one."

"That much? Why, because you black?"

"Only thing I can figure." He did not look up. It was as if someone had tied big slabs of stone to his arms.

George sighed. "No wonder nobody can do nothing to get better houses."

"I got me four grand left in the bank from fighting and from saving some of my salary each week, but that ain't enough. Besides, it wouldn't leave me nothing to work with to fix the places up."

George turned and took the steak off the grill, dripping it onto a blue plate. "What kind vegetables you want?"

"What you got?"

"Peas and carrots and mashed."

"Uh, gimme the peas and the mashed."

"I tell you," George said as he set the plate in front of A.L., "maybe there is another way. I could go to the same bank and buy the houses for maybe one thousand down apiece." He watched A.L. closely as he said it, knowing the feeling of defeat his offer would generate. He saw it rise with a tightening of the cords in the heavy neck and then subside. "We could form a corporation. You put in one thousand to match me and we go fifty-fifty on the costs and profits."

A.L. looked up slowly, his head cocked to one side. "You'd do that?"

"Sure, why not?" George set the plate of rolls behind the glass of beer. "Smart business to invest in the men you know. I see how you keep those bunch gangsters in line over there." He leaned against the counter behind him, crossing his arms over his chest. "How much is repairs going to cost?"

"They gotta be rewired and all the plumbing has to be taken out and the kitchens done over. Both houses need new roofs and they'll need some work on the porches and stuff, but all the floors are sound and those dirty furnaces work good enough."

"They both oil heat?"

"Uh-huh."

"Good. Here, gas cost too much."

A.L. scratched his temple under the hatband. "I figure four grand each ought to make them into real nice places."

"Can you raise another thousand?"

"I can save that much in two months, if I keep on living like I am now."

"They paying you that much over there?"

"With the overtime."

"What the hell you want to go into this for? You making good money now."

"I don't know, I guess I'm tired of being pushed around. Having places of my own could maybe make a difference. Besides, what's gonna happen when I get too old to beat those bastards into line? I don't figure to get kicked upstairs, just out."

George walked off down the bar to draw two beers for his customers and another for A.L.

"I tell you what," he said as he sat down on his stool, "I got to see my lawyer tomorrow about something else and I'll bring it up and maybe have him draw up the papers. You get your thousand and we'll close the deal tomorrow when you come in for supper. Okay?"

"You mean just like that?"

"Sure, why not?"

"George, you have made yourself a deal." A.L.'s grin spread in a flash of white beneath his broad nose. "You have made yourself a deal, man."

They shook hands, both smiling. "You know that kid you was asking about?" A.L. said.

"What about him?"

"I was thinking of putting him to work for me part time once we get started. He might even finish school, somebody pushes him a little."

12

BILLY OAKES walked out of the tunnel into the warm spring sun just as it burst through the fog bank that had crept down over the city during the night. The air was still damp and strangely chill and he buttoned his jacket tightly, right to the throat. He walked slowly, following along the river bank and up into the city, his hands curled into the pockets of his denim jacket.

It was three days now since he had been out of the tunnel and the brightness hurt his eyes, making him squint. Once again the people had changed. No one talked and they looked at him sideways, even as they looked at each other, their eyes dodging down when he caught them. The men walked quickly through the morning, at times seeming ready to run, anxious to get off the street and into the shelter of the buildings.

Billy did not hurry but walked easily along as he usually did. Before, his pace had kept him with the crowds of people. Now it left him lagging behind almost as if he were purposefully dawdling. He did not realize at first that it was his slow pace that caused them to look, to notice him, as if asking why he wasn't hurrying with them.

He picked up the pace, keeping up with them, and they stopped looking. He could feel himself starting to sweat, and he started worrying about his scent, but if he slowed down the eyes beat at him like branches in a windy forest, forcing him to walk faster and faster until now he was looking for a way to get out of the stream, and when they passed an alley the stream bent out and away from it and he could not drop out without being spotted. Finally he turned onto a side street, the crowd thinner here but moving just as fast. He dropped off two steps and slipped into the first alley, leaning up against the side of the building, his breath coming in short hard gasps.

"Hey! What're you doing?" A voice floated down the alley at him from the downhill end of the alley. He ran. He turned out of the alley and ran before the cop could fire, turned himself loose and ran blindly, without any direction or purpose until suddenly he could smell the river thick in his flaring nostrils. The people were staring at him openly now as he fled past. It was like running from a swarm of bees, and the more corners he turned the safer he felt. He did not know that the cop had not chased him.

The buildings gave way to a wild criss-crossing series of roadways and railroad tracks. He crossed on one of the bridges and turned in through an area where they were building, finally slowing to a walk, heading up and along the river bank and back to the tunnel.

He sat inside the pile of crates, staring through the dim light. If he stayed here in the tunnel he could only come out at night. He was afraid of the law, and they were all stirred up now. Even his father had not tried to fight the law. They had too much on their side.

There was enough money in the roll to last him awhile. He could wait it out here. Besides, if he left the tunnel it would be hard to find another place so close to Daniel's. But maybe the best thing was just to follow the river and stay away from here for a while. Once things calmed down he could come back. But now it was even dangerous to go buy food.

He waited for dark before going out again. Without hesitating he turned and followed the river downstream. At first he walked along old torn-up streets at the edge of the downtown area, blocked from the river edge by a solid wall of old brown buildings. At the huge waterfall he had to detour, walking along the edge of the cliff, the water nearly a hundred feet below. About a thousand yards beyond the falls the land began to slope steadily down toward the water, and he scrambled over discarded tires and rubble until he reached the water's edge.

Even with the debris it was better walking. There were no people and no tracks of anyone having been there since the water had begun to drop. It reminded him of home and the rivers that ran down out of the mountains.

The land grew steadily wilder though the dirty smell of the river, and the constant smoke, sharp and thick, kept him alert and aware of the danger. Once he pasted himself against a tree, holding his breath as two dogs dashed past in the dark, hot on the heels of a rabbit. He had thought they might be after him until he heard them bay and knew it was a rabbit.

By midnight he had reached a point where the river banks flattened and there were boats and people along the sides of the river. He had never seen so many or such big boats, and he could not understand why they were all gathered in one spot.

He moved back from the river edge to where a line of empty freight cars stood. It was dark and shadowy there and he moved fast, crouching along until he came to the end of the big boxcars. Then, standing upright, he braved the open for the hundred yards to where boats were up on land.

The boats here were dark and he decided they would make a good place to hole up. He walked in and around the darkened hulls looking for one which showed no signs of people. Suddenly his nostrils flared and he froze into the dark. The smell drifted past and he waited and moved on, stopping when it drifted in again on a light breeze, and then walking faster in the dead air between the puffs of wind. When it was gone, he knew he had passed upwind of it and he doubled back, watching carefully. He stopped beside a boat, looking at the lines of even holes stitched across the hull. The wood was fresh where it had splintered around the edges of each hole.

He moved on quickly, walking out onto the railroad tracks, careless in his anxiety to leave the smell and the boat with the holes in its side.

He could see a tall bridge in the distance with cars streaming both ways over it. Down below on the tracks it was dark and it looked safe, but he was feeling more and more uneasy at having left the safety of his tunnel. Good places were hard to find, and he had been lucky to find the tunnel. Billy kept moving, passing up an old railroad station that hung on the edge of the lights. With the tracks on one side and the boats tied on the other, it left no place to run except the river itself. He stayed with the tracks, leaving them when they crossed to the west side of the road. He stopped and studied a tall stone tower and then moved on. It was too open and the grass around it had been cut recently.

The tracks ended abruptly at the river just where he crossed them again. He stood looking at the big black swing bridge in the middle of the river, not understanding why the tracks ended or how the trains could cross with the bridge pointing in the direction of the current.

Down at the bottom of the south embankment he spotted a small gray shack. It looked abandoned, one end hanging out over the river on thick piles. He slid on down the crushed-stone side, trying not to disturb it but still sending a few stones clattering ahead of him.

The windows were heavily screened and the door had a large brass padlock on it. He eased around to the water side, wading out knee-deep, and after looking carefully around, ducked under the building. He pulled out his knife and began working on the rotted floor boards, splitting them apart easily, and in minutes he was inside and comfortably settled.

He ate the food he had brought and then rolled into his

blanket and dropped instantly into his sound, undreaming sleep.

During the night the river began to rise slowly but steadily under the pressure of a sudden downpour. Before, during a heavy rain the water had risen to the floor of the shack, but the boards swollen with the dampness had kept the water out. Now with the hole in the floor it ran in unresisted, waking Billy and driving him up into the rafters.

13

A.L. SAT with his dirty boots propped on the kitchen table, his steel hat tipped forward to shield his eyes from the naked glare of the single overhead bulb. He was drunk and his big arms were crossed over his chest to keep them from slipping and hanging uncomfortably at his sides. He was smiling, tight-lipped, almost as if he were afraid to show his teeth. He had always known George was soul, and tomorrow night when those papers were signed he would have a chance to stick it to all those white bastards who had stuck it to him and all the rest of the black men, those bastards who fucked him out of his career.

Inside, his happiness roared like a bonfire. One time, baby, that's all I'm asking, he thought. Just one time to wear them businessman's rags and a white shirt and tie and some fifty-dollar kicks so that maybe broads like the one he'd seen in the street would be giving him a tumble instead of chasing after those toms. Just one time, man, ohhhh baby! He hugged himself, squeezing hard, and then threw back his head and laughed in one roaring bellow. He laughed again and then the laugh trailed into a high-pitched shriek. It would be even better than fighting, because sooner or later somebody would have come along and pounded him and he'd of wound up all scarred and ugly. This here was a different game. Wouldn't nobody be pounding on his head, trying to get into his pocket, thinking maybe he was some dumb nigger. This time they had a surprise coming, yessir!

He felt warm all over, the way he had as a kid wandering naked down the summer beach in Savannah. He unwrapped his arms and stuffed his big hands into the pockets of his mud-stained work pants. The chair creaked beneath him, the old glue crumbling in the joints when he moved or shifted. It was a miracle it held him up at all.

Downstairs he could hear one of Hews's kids crying. The sound diminished slowly, but the thought had taken root and he followed it further, wondering what a white southern boy was doing living in a rat hole like this, and a rat hole full of black people to boot. Maybe he just couldn't afford nothing else? That had to be it, because there wasn't any other reason that would explain it.

Down on the street he could hear Henry Jones and one of his wine-drinking brothers coming home laughing in the high-pitched way that was always a thing for white bastards to laugh at. He slipped lightly off the chair and went over to the window, looking down through the dirty panes without bending as Henry and his buddy staggered by, holding each other up. The flash of light, a sliver of brightness, came just before the bottle crashed against the street. A.L. shook his head. What else was there for them? He started as his eyes picked off another flash over the abandoned house. He watched carefully, holding his breath to listen for the slightest sound. There was nothing except the laughter rolling out of the two drunks, no movement in the house or around it. "Jus' your imagination," he said aloud, but he kept looking and then went back and clicked off the light so he could see out without being silhouetted against the window. Nothing.

He yawned, the booze making him sleepy now. He'd better

get some sleep so he'd be awake when they signed the papers. Couldn't have that lawyer thinking he was dumb.

He stripped down to his underwear and fell onto the bed, not bothering with the blanket rumpled at his feet. It was warm in the apartment. He lay on his back staring up at the ceiling, thinking about that tall broad. He could see her walking away from him down the street, that fine, round ass twitching slowly, temptingly like the switch of a thin-shanked racehorse. He thought about what she would look like naked, whether her breasts would stand up or whether it was her bra that kept them pointed out. The young broad he had brought up here the night before had those real firm young breasts that he liked, but she was dumb and just good for fucking and nothing else. He wanted a woman.

Four members of the detective bureau goon squad woke A.L. at three A.M., breaking apart the pieces of a dream he did not want to surrender. Even in the dark he knew who they were.

"Time to get up," one of them said, his voice vaguely taunting.

A.L. pulled himself up and sat on the edge of the bed. "What you want?"

"Just a few questions," the same voice said.

"Come back in the morning," A.L. said, swinging his feet back up onto the bed.

"Get up, nigger!" A different voice, stronger and more threatening.

A.L. sat up again and swung his feet out onto the floor, wishing he had not had those three extra drinks the night before, wishing there was a way to avoid having to get out of bed in the middle of the night and talk to a bunch of stupid cops and lose the sleep he would need the next day at work.

"Okay, what you want?" he asked, looking down at the floor as he rubbed the top of his head.

"Get your clothes on." That was Kelly.

A.L. looked up. "What for?"

"You wanna go down to headquarters bare-ass?"

"What you busting me for? I ain't done nothing!" He could feel the frustration slowly changing to anger and he tried to control it, knowing the worst thing he could do was give them the chance to bust him for resisting arrest.

Now in the dark he could make out Pellegrini. He was the biggest of the bunch but the most dangerous was Kelly, known all over town as a nigger-hater who sometimes picked up some cat and bounced him around the station just for kicks. He stood up and pulled his pants on, moving very slowly as he tried to wake himself up and start thinking.

"Hurry up," Kelly ordered.

A.L. took his time, even in going out to the car, dawdling as much as they'd allow, trying to remember what he might have done, outside of being drunk occasionally.

They took him right up to the fourth floor and then back to the isolation room at the end of the detention cells where they held people for questioning. They locked him in the room with Kelly and Pellegrini and one other detective he didn't know. The third man stood over by the door, out of the light.

"Sit here," Pellegrini said, pointing to the chair in the center of the room beneath the shaded light.

A.L. sat down, his hands dangling between his knees as he looked up at the two detectives, his eyes still heavy with sleep.

"You want to tell us about it?" Kelly asked from behind the barrier of bright light.

"Tell you about what?"

"The murders?"

"What murders?"

"Let me put it another way," Kelly said. "You can either tell us now, or you can play dumb and we'll beat it out of you.

We know you got a motive for killing all those white men. We got a team of men searching your apartment now for the knife. We also got two witnesses who say they saw you leaving the scene of the last killing."

"Man, you cop bastards are really something, you know that? I mean just because I'm black and I been in the pen, you gonna try and pin everything on me. I got a good job and I make plenty of dough and I ain't broke one single fucking law!"

"Look, nigger, we know what your record is," Kelly said. "And we know you hate white men, boy."

He kept saying to himself over and over and over, cool it! Don't let them get to you. Keep cool. If they needle you into a fight here, they can shoot your black ass dead and won't nobody give half a shit. Better to play dumb-ass, let those cop bastards play their game, and then beat them at it. If they had anything on you they wouldn't have you here asking a bunch of damn fool questions.

"Anytime you're ready, nigger," Kelly said, "we got a stenographer right outside."

"You arresting me?"

"You know that ain't necessary," Kelly said. "We are just having us a little talk first."

A.L. decided not to say another word, to just sit there in the bright light and wait for them to move.

After nearly five minutes, Pellegrini said, "You want me to work him over a little?"

"Yeah, but don't hit him where it'll show too bad."

Pellegrini walked into the light, smiling at A.L. as he approached and then stepped off to the side to get some leverage.

A.L. suddenly realized they had forgotten to handcuff him to the chair, and he knew now that no matter whether it was a trap or not he couldn't take being hit and without the handcuffs he at least had a chance to mess them up.

The first blow Pellegrini landed was an openhanded slap, catching A.L. high on the cheekbone as he rolled with it and then exploded up out of the chair, his left fist pile-driving into the man's gut, bending him into his right hand chopping down. He held him up to use as a shield should Kelly pull his gun. He could feel the warmth of blood on his fingers and he realized he must have hit the tin shade on the light because it was swinging back and forth in a crazy, eccentric arc and he couldn't find Kelly. As he turned he heard the move and ducked and the blackjack banged off his shoulder, and he let go of Pellegrini and back-handed Kelly into the far wall just as the third man pushed the alarm button on the wall inside the door. He crossed the room with two strides and grabbed the man by the shoulder, spinning him around into a right cross that broke his jaw in two places.

A.L. stood by the door waiting for the pounding feet coming rapidly closer. He let the first one get through the door and then lowered the boom on him, whirling fast to hit the next man with a one-two combination that flattened his nose in a shower of blood.

Bells were ringing now all through the building and he could hear cops shouting and running around. He clobbered one more detective and a uniformed man before the blast of a gun in the small room seemed to explode his eardrums and he felt the sudden burst of pain in his leg and then it was just numb and wet and hot with blood. He did not go down but reeled into the hall, coming face to face with Chief Barton and a young man with a mustache and a notebook. A.L. slid quietly to the floor, weak now, his entire trouser leg soaked with blood.

It wasn't long before he could hear the ambulances. At least now he would be in the hospital and he'd be able to get a lawyer. And they'd have to come up with a reason for having taken him down to the station and questioned him without his even being booked.

14

EVER SINCE early afternoon, when one of the guys said he heard on the radio that the stabber was caught, Daniel had hardly been able to stand still in front of his machine. Twice he ruined pieces by putting too much pressure on the cutting tool and gouging the bright aluminum. No one was there to notice, and he just heaved the ruined castings into the scrap barrel and took another from the wooden box next to his machine.

If he had a dime he could have bought a paper on the way out of the shop to read on the bus, but he had only the quarter to get home. There were no extra papers on the bus, though all around him the people talked excitedly, their voices still strained but some of the fear and edginess gone.

He tried to shut out their words, wanting to read about it himself without hearing about it first. Once or twice he thought he heard them use a name which was familiar, but he could not make it out for sure.

Once off the bus he broke into an easy trot, his heavy, muscled legs carrying him easily along and his thick black hair flopping in counter rhythm to the thud of his work shoes on the pavement. He burst through the gate and into the house. Fumbling for his key, he dropped it, picked it up and tried to put it in upside down, swore, got it into the lock, and turned it the wrong way. Finally he got it right and the door opened with a soft click. He slammed it behind him, picking the paper off the end table where Sarah had set it and dropping into the chair, his lunch pail in his lap as he read.

STABBER SUBDUED AFTER BEATING SEVEN COPS

The alleged stabber, according to police, is ex-prizefighter A. L. Smith, of 421 Clarissa St.

Daniel looked up from the paper. The guy upstairs? He'd been living right in the same house with the guy, had passed him in the hall, had talked to him!

"Daniel? Is that you?" Sarah called from the kitchen.

"Uh-huh."

"What are you doing?"

"Reading the paper."

She walked into the living room, wiping her hands on a kitchen towel. "What's so important?"

"Nothing." He didn't know whether she knew about the stabber. They seldom watched the news, and she still wasn't able to read the paper.

"Then what are you so excited about?"

"Nothing. Just heard a rumor at the factory about some new jobs opening up. There was supposed to be a story about it in the paper."

She didn't believe him and he knew he was going to have to tell her, but not now. He looked down at the paper and she walked back to the kitchen.

Smith is now in the prison ward of the County Hospital with a gunshot wound in his left leg.

According to police, Smith was shot after he went berserk during routine questioning and severely beat seven detectives.

Smith's arrest, Police Chief Lemuel Barton said today, was

the result of a "long and thorough investigation and involved a lot of plain, old-fashioned detective work."

According to Barton, four detectives from "A" Squad took Smith into custody at his Clarissa Street apartment shortly after three A.M.

It was during the brief questioning session which followed at police headquarters that Smith allegedly went "berserk" and attacked detectives.

"He's an ex-prizefighter," Chief Barton said, "and very strong (Smith stands six feet six inches and weighs close to 250 pounds), but we didn't want to shoot him unless it was a last resort. The interrogation room is small and there wasn't room to hold him. When he tried to escape, one of the detectives shot him in the leg."

Smith, when he is released from the hospital, will be charged with the murders of five men. He can be tried separately on each count of first degree murder, according to Chief Barton.

Daniel folded the paper in half and dropped it on the table, then walked out into the kitchen with his lunch pail. He set it on the sink next to where Sarah was washing some pots and pans, retreated to the table, and lit a cigarette.

"I lied to you just now about what I was looking for in the paper," he said.

"I know." She stood with her back to him, her hands on the edge of the sink.

"I lied because I didn't want to tell you and get you upset for nothing. There's been a murderer loose in the city for close to a month now and they finally caught him."

"What's that got to do with anything?"

"You knew about the killer?"

"I heard about it on the radio. That's all they been talking about for weeks."

"You know the man they arrested is that big nigger that lives upstairs?"

"Daniel, why'd you lie and why didn't you kiss me when you came home? You never forgot before."

He walked over and stood behind her, putting his arms around her waist gently, afraid to squeeze. "C'mon, sit down." He led her over to the table and sat across from her. "I don't think the man upstairs is the killer. I think it's Billy or Jake Oakes. Probably Billy."

He could see the fear explode in her eyes and feel her hard shudder. "Daniel, don't say that. It couldn't be. Billy's way down Georgia and Jake's in prison."

"I think Billy's here. I been followed at least twice and I know when it's an Oakes that's tracking me. They got a certain way just like a ghost that you can never catch at it. I wrote to Aunt May to find out if Billy's still there."

"Did you get an answer?"

"Not yet."

"Why don't you go to the police?"

He folded his hands together, bending them in toward his chest until the knuckles cracked. "I can't."

She leaned toward him. "For heaven's sake why not?"

"You remember when Charlie Clay got hisself killed? It was Billy done it. I saw him. I was standing there and I couldn't do nothing. I always been afraid that if I ever told anybody he'd come after me or maybe after you and the kids." Daniel's dark eyes seemed dull, covered with a cloudy film. "If I was to go to the police, just sure'n'hell Billy'd come after me."

"How'd he know?"

"Them Oakes always know. You know you can't hide nothing from an Oakes."

"Well, it just don't matter this time. We ain't living in Georgia! You got to go to the police."

"I will if that letter comes from Aunt May and she says he ain't there. But the risk is too big unless I'm sure he's here. You understand, Sarah?"

"No. It don't make any sense!"

"If I go to the police and they catch Billy and he tells 'em how I seen him kill Charlie Clay and didn't do nothing, they'll put me in jail too."

"What for?"

"For not turning in Billy before." He ran his right hand through his hair. "To the police it's almost the same as if I done it myself."

"Oh, God, Daniel, why?" She was starting to cry.

"I bought a gun," he said. "If I see Billy I'll kill him."

"Daniel, you can't. Then the police will come after you for sure."

"No, not for killing him to save myself. And he won't be able to talk and tell about before."

"Please go to the police," Sarah said. "Please."

"No, at least not until the letter comes."

"Then?"

"Yes, then."

15

In the morning Billy climbed down out of the rafters. The floor was still wet, but looking out through the hole he could see that the river had dropped enough so he could get out of the shack.

He walked around the inside, stopping at each window, checking carefully, listening for any sound. It was quiet and outside he could not see anyone. Across the river there was some activity, but it was far enough away so that they would not notice him in the dark below the shack. He dropped out through the hole and waded ashore onto the large boulders.

The sun was just coming up and he found a spot where he could sit without much chance of being seen and where he could see the bridge that did not touch the shore. A soft mist moved across the river, coming faster as the sun climbed slowly up into a clear sky.

The sun was warm and it felt fine to just sit there soaking it up. It was the first time he had been able to sit this way without having to keep completely alert. He had not realized how wet the tunnel and the shack had been until now and he could feel the dampness frying out of his clothes and his skin.

He watched a big boat coming up the river. It was the biggest boat he had ever seen and as it came closer he could see people moving around like wood ants on the back end of it, coming and going from a large house.

Billy watched until it went around a bend in the river and disappeared, leaving only the waves it had pushed up slithering in and around the rocks. The sun made him think of home again and he wondered how his dogs were. He had raised them from pups and there were no better dogs around. His mother was probably not feeding them regular enough, and he wondered if they would still be there when he got back or if they would have run off into the woods to hunt for themselves. They were big and fast and they could run for days. He shook his head slowly from side to side as he looked out at the bridge. There was so much here he didn't understand.

He reached down and felt his pants where they had been wet. They were completely dry now and even his boots were nearly dry. He stood up and climbed the rest of the way up onto the tracks, walking back the way he had come. He liked it much better here. There were fewer people and he didn't have to watch and listen so hard.

He noticed two cars parked at the stone tower and was glad he had not tried to get in there last night. The shack was fine for a while. He could sit inside, and anybody checking around would look at the door and the windows and leave.

Up the first side street he came to, Billy found a grocery store that had just opened for the day. He walked in, trying to look relaxed and calm.

"Hello," the woman at the register said.

Billy nodded back. "Hello."

He walked to the back of the store to the meat case and picked out a couple of steaks and some of the stuff that came in slices. He bought some bread too and then stood waiting as the woman rang it up.

"That'll be eight-fifty," she said.

Billy peeled a ten off the roll of money and gave it to her.

"Thank you," she said.

"Uh-huh."

"You new around here?" Her voice was warm and friendly.

"Uh-huh." He picked up the bag.

"Where you staying?"

"With my cousin," he said. He did not like her questions, but somehow, the way she asked them, it didn't seem like she was being nosy. He headed for the door.

"Have a nice day," she said.

"Thank you."

As he walked, holding the bag and the loaf of bread with his left arm, Billy tore off chunks of bread with his teeth and stuffed some of the cold meat into his mouth along with the bread. A breeze had come up and tossed and toyed with his hair, rippling it in the sunlight.

He was relaxed and thinking how good the food tasted, and his distraction allowed the tall, dark man to come up on him from behind, to get within a step of him before Billy felt him there and whirled into a crouch as the bag of groceries fell to the pavement.

"What're you doing here, kid?"

Billy stood absolutely still. He heard the other man coming up behind and he could see him clearly reflected in the dark glasses of the man in front of him. Slowly he relaxed, straightening back up, hoping they would relax too. He heard the double click of the gun hammer but he held himself in check, trying to judge what was going on behind him by the face of the man in front. There was no danger yet.

"What y'all want?" Billy asked.

"Just want to know what you're doing here."

"Nothing. I just bought me some food over to the store."

The man in front nodded and the one behind lowered the gun. It was wide open here and he would be an easy target if he tried to run. He had to work his way toward the boxcars that stood some twenty feet away.

"Whattya think?" one of them asked.

"Tony said to bring him up to the tower if we had any doubt."

The only thing Billy could figure was that he must have been trespassing. But he hadn't seen any signs. In fact he couldn't remember having seen a single No Trespassing sign since he left Georgia.

"He's just a kid."

The one in front looked at him carefully, staring at him through the dark glasses. Billy waited, leaving the bag of groceries on the ground where it had fallen.

"I don't know. There's something about him that makes me think we ought to let Tony decide, but I don't wanna hear a bunch of shit about being stupid and wasting his time."

"I'd rather take some shit than make a mistake," the man behind him said.

"Yeah I guess you're right. C'mon with us, kid, we want you to meet a friend of ours." He motioned toward the tower.

Billy turned slowly. The tower was not a good place to get caught and if he was going to run it would have to be now. He stooped to pick up his grocery bag as the man who had been behind him came up next to him, putting one of the men on each side. He smoothed his hair, sliding his right hand to the back of his neck.

Then he moved, the big knife slashing like a snake's tongue, laying open the neck of the man on his right and coming around to bury itself in the chest of the man with the dark glasses.

Billy yanked the knife free and ran for the boxcars, getting them between himself and the tower and sprinting toward the line of big sheds along the water. There the tower was out of sight, its view cut off by a shallow bluff, and he kept running, holding his pace at the top of his speed, making the last corner and clambering quickly down over the rocks and under the edge of the shack and inside, sprawling flat on the damp floor to catch his wind.

In less than a half-hour he heard people outside and he slipped up onto the rafters, standing back up against the gable where the shadows were the deepest. Two of them tried the iron grates on the windows and rattled the big padlock on the door.

"Nothing here," one of them said.

"We ain't gonna find nothing either."

"You think Tony's right?"

"What do you think? We knocked off that punk this winter and then they got Reed. So we shoot up three of them and they hit us back."

"They must have had a boat waiting."

"Yeah, what else."

Close to midnight Billy heard an engine cough into life out on the bridge. He dropped down out of the shack, watching as the bridge swung slowly toward the shore. Far up on the tracks he heard a train pitching its high wail into the humid night. When the train moved past, he scrambled up the bank and hitched a ride across. Just down over the embankment there was a row of old, broken boats. He found one with a big hole in the bottom and crawled through. He could stay until morning, anyway. He had not been so hungry since he had been cooped up in that boxcar with all the paper.

16

THE GUARDS at the hospital reminded George of the times back in Greece when he had been under guard as a political prisoner. They made him nervous, but his lawyer Craig Morton did the talking and there was no trouble.

"Hey, prizefighter!" George said as he stuck his head around the door, "how you get yourself into this? Huh?"

"Hey, George," A.L. said. He grinned broadly, his teeth big and white against his black skin. "What you doing here?"

"I hear they got my partner in jail for murders which I know he didn't do because he was sitting in my place drinking when two of them was committed, so I come to see if I can't get him out." He motioned back toward the tall dark-suited man. "I even brought my lawyer Mr. Morton to help."

Craig Morton, young, with black hair and blue eyes, nodded at A.L.

"Glad to know you, Mr. Morton," A.L. said. "Why don't you two grab some chairs and sit down?"

George and Craig moved the two chairs next to the bed, down toward the end where A.L. could see them easily.

"Now," George said, "how come they grab you?" His pudgy features folded into a frown.

"Ahh, it was the goon squad, man. They come and drag me

out of bed and down to the station and start asking a lot of questions about the murders trying to get me to confess, and when I wouldn't they got rough and I decided I wasn't gonna sit there and let them knock me around, especially Kelly."

"Yeah, that Kelly," George said. He sat with his knees spread, a hand on each knee, his elbows out.

A.L. grinned again. "Be a while before he gets back into action."

"What'd they arrest you on when they were at your apartment?" Craig asked.

"Nothing."

"They just dragged you down to the station house?"

"That's right. They can always think up something if they have to."

"Hey," George said, "how is the leg?"

"Not too bad. The doctor told me the bullet just went through the muscle, didn't hit no bone or nothing. He says I oughta be up tomorrow and walking on it by Friday."

"That's when they've got the hearing scheduled," Craig said.

"Uh-huh."

"Huh! We have you out by then," George said.

"Well, maybe we will, George," Craig said. "Let me explain it this way." He looked down and then back up at A.L. "There's something peculiar about this whole thing. I talked to the District Attorney this morning after George called me, but he wouldn't tell me much. Now I've known Pete for years and I've watched him in court often enough to know that when he has a case he never hesitates. But this morning I had the feeling that he hasn't got much. Now, it may be that he just hasn't got it all together yet, but it could also mean that in fact he hasn't got a case. One thing sure, there's some pressure somewhere."

A.L. stirred uneasily, suddenly aware of the pain in his leg. "I don't know what he could have," he said.

"Here's the problem we face," Craig said. "George's alibi won't hold up in court."

"What you mean!" George said, a frown deepening the already heavy lines in his face.

"The night Stein was killed you say A.L. was there at your place. But you close at two and Stein was killed just after two only a block away." He opened his attaché case and pulled out a long yellow pad on which he had scribbled some notes.

"George told me you have some money saved up, is that right?"

"Yeah, that's right, about four thousand."

"Well they could be trying to connect that with the money that was stolen from each of the victims."

"I can prove where I got that money from. Half of it was from before I went to prison and the rest I saved from working."

"I have to admit it's pretty weak evidence. Not many killers keep savings accounts for the money they steal, and I don't think this one even stole very much, but I have to try and anticipate every argument they may have. Can you prove where that money came from?"

"I told you I can. I get paid every week on Thursday and I put the money in my account at Central. They been cashing my checks for close to two years there."

"Do you keep any money around your apartment?"

"No. The most I ever carry is twenty dollars." He looked up, his eyes narrowing. "You think they planted some dough there?"

"They could have. I know there's a lot of trouble at police headquarters over this. You put seven men out of action, you know, and that leaves a lot of questions without answers."

"I don't know what to tell you, Mr. Morton. I ain't killed nobody. I know that. George knows that, but ain't no way I can prove it."

"What's that talk, huh? He's innocent till they prove he's not, huh?"

Craig shook his head as he slipped the note pad back into the tan case. "I just wish I knew what in hell is going on. I heard this morning from my contact inside the D.A.'s office that three men were machine-gunned up in the north end the other night."

"Machine-gunned?" A.L. said.

"Sounds like Greece," said George.

"None of the pieces seem to fit together," Craig said, "but I think there's a way to put some pressure on Pete to find out just where we stand. I think it's a pretty good guess that he hasn't got a case and he's hoping they'll come up with enough by Friday to keep them all from looking too bad. Maybe if he thought I was going to file a false arrest suit he'd have to find a way to talk me out of it. It's a gamble, but at this point I don't know what else to do."

"It don't look too good, does it?" A.L. said.

"Huh!" George said. "What we need is the killer to kill someone else. What kind of a thing is that? They got an innocent man in jail and somebody else has to die for him to go free."

"Well, I don't think it's that bad," Craig said, "but I have to admit it wouldn't hurt our case one bit."

When they were gone A.L. slid down as deeply into the bed as he could, staring up at the neat, even rows of holes in the ceiling. What pissed him off most, he decided, was that he hadn't got to bust up that motherfucker Barton while he was at it.

17

IN THE MORNINGS during the next two days Billy sat inside the cabin of his new home watching the parade in and out of the tower across the river. He had been able to steal some food from some of the boats that were in the water, but every time it was a risk. There were too many lights. Out the side window he could see the masts of several boats sticking up over the railroad embankment, and he decided that after dark he would look for food over there.

Once he left he could not come back. They were still looking for him on the other side of the river, and it would not be long before they began looking over here. He would go back to the tunnel.

During the later afternoon it rained steadily beneath a gray and thickly clouded sky, tufted like a sofa.

He sat in the vinyl chair behind the old ship's wheel, watching the rain and the water streaming down the glass windshield. His boat was higher than any of the others around and he could see easily between the crystal beads of water on the side windows. The rain seemed to close him in, seal him off, and he wanted to move but he could not, his instinct telling him to wait. He slid to the edge of the chair and began working himself into the sort of suspended state which his father had taught him and which allowed him to wait.

By dark it was still raining and Billy tucked his collar tightly around his neck and then dropped out through the hole in the boat and into the open. He paused, listening, holding his breath. He heard nothing unusual, nothing which set him up, and he looked around once quickly before walking out into the clearing and over the embankment.

On the other side the brush was thick and he wormed through it carefully, picking his way, making hardly a sound. He broke out of the brush near the docks, crouching low as he looked over the rows of boats, bobbing softly in their slips.

The nearest dock was at least twelve feet from shore, separated by a sluggish stretch of water in which old tires and empty cans and bottles floated. The entrance ramp was two hundred yards away and brightly lit.

Billy walked along the bank until he found a tree the right height and thickness and then climbed up quickly as it sagged out over the water, depositing him onto the dock next to a large, square-backed boat.

He had not realized how many lights there were on the dock and he slunk down low, keeping his profile as close to the planks as he could.

The boat was dark. From the back he would have chosen another, but he did not like staying on the dock in the open with only the water behind him. He slipped up over the gunwale and into the large cockpit, holding himself frozen, listening, and then finally moving toward the door. The air smelled suddenly sweet and it stopped him next to the cabin door until it blew by. The rain had stopped—in an hour it would be clear.

He slipped the knife into the door jamb and pushed back the pin on the lock and stepped softly down into the curtained dark, shutting the door behind him. Then he froze: held by the sweet smell of a woman. There was a purse on the table and he picked it up, opening it carefully. A movement in the dark made him crouch quickly down close to the cabin floor and the cabin wall.

Now he could see her lying on top of one of the bunks. She was naked, tossing in her sleep. He stared at her body, watching the way it lifted gently with her breathing, her tits glistening with sweat in the damp heat. He moved closer, longing to touch her, to feel the soft smooth skin the way he had with Sarah Ann. She was young and her tits were big. He reached out slowly in the dark, touching them, as she rolled onto her back. He jerked his hand away and waited, then touched them again, this time letting his hand wander down over her body, finally burying itself between her legs. She spread herself slowly and he jerked his hand back. He couldn't tell whether she was awake or not. She didn't seem to be, but he couldn't see how she could be asleep now. Still, he'd better not touch her again. If she woke he would have to kill her, even though he didn't want to.

He emptied the wallet in her purse and stuffed the money into the pocket of his dungarees, keeping the knife ready even as he backed toward the door, watching her until his hand touched the handle of the door behind him. Her breathing seemed even and steady and he opened the door and stepped outside.

He started down the dock, walking straight toward the lights at the end as a big man suddenly stepped out of the shadows, coming off one of the finger piers, and rammed right into him, staggering back as he squinted into the dark to see who it was. The smell of whiskey was strong in the damp air.

"Hey," he said, "why don't you look where you're going?"

Billy drove the knife straight into his heart, catching him as he fell. He had taken the man's money and was cleaning off his knife when the woman in the boat began to scream. He ran, the knife still in his hand, flying through the night, his feet thumping against the hollow dock. Even as he ran he saw a man step into the light at the end of the pier and look up the dock toward him. The woman screamed again and Billy burst out of the dark, knocking the man into a shed wall as he flew past.

He did not know where to run or which way to go and he did not dare stop, just hurled himself along the road until he could twist off through a field full of rubble. He slowed down just long enough to see the junk. If he tripped or hurt a leg he would be through. He ran toward a big shed; rounding it, he saw the bridge lit up against the night. He headed for it, knowing that the tracks would be near there and that once he found them he could get back to the tunnel.

He stopped below the bridge, looking across at the tracks on the other side. The only way was over the top. Next to a small shack a big dog started to bark, and a light flicked on inside the shack.

Billy walked to where he could climb onto the iron beams beneath the roadway of the bridge. Slowly he began inching out. The vibration from the cars and trucks rattling along above him threatened to loosen his hold at times, but his hands were dry and he had never been bothered by high places.

Near the middle there were no beams for his feet and he slung himself across, hand over hand, reaching up over the main beams to grab the struts where he could get a firm grip. Here the bridge was different, and it moved every time a car crossed, swaying slightly, and when a big trailer truck crossed it nearly knocked him loose, leaving him dangling by one hand, his face screwed into a grimace as he held and waited.

Once over the middle section the rest was easy, and when he climbed down he was standing on the tracks. He turned down them back toward the city, breaking into an easy trot.

18

DANIEL FOUND the letter in the mailbox when he came home from work. The address was plainly and neatly written, so Aunt May must have got someone to write it for her, probably the preacher or one of her customers.

He tore it open, still standing in the narrow hall, the sun streaming in hot through the windows opened to the afternoon.

> DEAR DANIEL,
>
> This letter is being written for me by Jason Coombs, who runs the feed store. I haven't seen Billy since early this spring. He just got himself up early one morning and disappeared and he ain't been back not even to feed his dogs. If you see him, tell him to come home because I got enough to do without having to tend to his fool hounds. His father is still in jail.
>
> *Love,*
>
> Aunt May

Daniel stuffed the letter into his shirt pocket and went inside, setting his lunch pail inside the door and walking out into the kitchen. He thought about the gun upstairs in his dresser and how glad he was now that he had bought it, that it was loaded and ready to use.

"Hi, honey," he said, coming up and kissing Sarah on the neck.

"Hi, sweet," she said, "how was work?"

He sat down at the white table. "Fine."

"Mrs. Clarke came today," Sarah said.

"She teaching you anything?"

"Uh-huh."

"Don't worry, honey," he said. "It's slow at first."

She turned and looked at him as she finished cutting the carrots into a pan of water. "That's what she told me. She said that once I learn the first books I can go to a class and I can even bring the kids along and somebody'll take care of them while I'm in class."

"Is that free too?"

"Uh-huh." She crossed the kitchen, smiling as she wiped her hands on her apron and sat down across from him.

Daniel took the letter from his pocket and dropped it on the table. "It's from Aunt May."

She looked at it, waiting for him to tell her what it said, her impatience revealing itself in the anxious flutter of her hands.

Daniel sat with his hands folded over each other on the smooth metal table. He had not decided yet and she knew it, and she also knew that she would have to wait and then go along with whatever he finally decided, whether she wanted to or not.

"Billy left home some time this spring. Aunt May don't say in the letter, but it might mean he's here."

"You gonna go to the police?"

"I don't know yet. If only I was sure it was Billy then I could take the chance. But what happens if it ain't and they start looking around and find out about what happened?"

"How they gonna find out unless they get it from Billy?"

He shook his head and then brushed the hair back up off his forehead. "He's here, I know he's here. I can feel him, even now, just the way I could when I was a kid and I knew he was somewhere out in the woods watching."

Daniel's glance caught the fear in her eyes. He reached out and took hold of her thin hand, squeezing it tightly. "I gotta think on it, Sarah, I just gotta have a little time to think on it."

"I know," she said, "but you promised after you got the letter. . . ." She looked down.

"I know, I promised I'd do something, and I will. I just gotta think on it awhile, figure out what's the best thing to do. Okay?"

"Okay."

"Now you just finish getting supper and I'll read the paper. Where's the kids?"

"Out back in the yard."

Daniel walked out the back door, pushing the flimsy screen door against the side of the house with a sharp slap. Inside Sarah could hear the joyful shouts of her children as they ran across the yard to see their father and almost immediately she began to cry, the tears blinding her so that she could hardly see the stove. She managed to get the heat turned down on the carrots and then wiped her eyes with her apron. She could remember Billy's hands that time at night, remember how slimy they felt as he ran them over her body, almost like a snake crawling over her while she lay there unable to move. He was horrible, he was insane, and he'd do anything because that's the way his father had raised him. Whatever he wanted he just took, and nobody came after him, not even the sheriff—because once Billy was off in the woods he did the hunting. She wished Daniel did not have to go to work. She was afraid even of being alone in the house, knowing that she would begin to jump with every sound and that the kids would feel her fear.

They all came through the door together, shouting and laughing as she stood there wiping her eyes.

"C'mon, into the living room," Daniel said as he herded them past his wife.

"Daddy, why is Mommy crying?"

"It's all right," she heard Daniel say, "she's just a little upset over something."

19

THAT AFTERNOON in the Midtown Mall, Billy Oakes, walking along listening to conversations he only partially understood, followed a group of people into the elevator.

He did not know where they were going and, distracted by their conversation, he just followed them in, assuming the door led to the outside. As the doors closed he backed into a corner of the elevator, his hands spread against the wall, his eyes bright with tension and his pulse pounding at his temples so loud he could barely hear. The people with their backs to him were not upset or nervous, continuing their talk as if nothing unusual were happening.

He waited and the room he was in began to rise, slowly at first and then picking up speed. Billy stayed tucked into the corner, waiting, ready now to go for his knife at the least sign. Only two of the people were talking, the others standing like cattle waiting at the barnyard gate. It seemed like hours before the room began to slow, and when it stopped the doors opened and one man left and two women walked in, turning their backs to him.

The doors closed and the elevator started to climb again. It climbed and then slowed and stopped, and a man came in and pushed against a little square that said 14. When he touched it the square lit up and they began to climb again. It stopped at number eight, and the men Billy had got on with left and several others walked on. When the number over the door read 14 the car stopped and everyone got out.

Billy followed them into a wide red hallway. The people walked away from him toward a large room and he stopped, watching them, unsure whether to follow or stay where he was. Almost involuntarily he walked a few yards further until he could see into the large room. There were huge windows on each side and as he looked out he could see the tops of buildings. It was like being on top of a mountain looking out over the tops of the trees. He walked into the big room, weaving his way through the tables and over to the window where he stood looking out over the city.

As he stood there, fascinated by the view, he heard a man come softly up behind him, and without looking around he picked up the reflection in the glass.

"Pardon me, sir." The voice was quiet behind him.

Billy did not turn but stood looking out, trying to put everything together in his mind. Suddenly he understood that he was inside one of the tall buildings he had looked up at from the ground, and that the little room was the way you got to the top of those buildings.

"Sir?"

Billy turned slowly and looked at the waiter, setting himself, ready for whatever might come next.

"I'm sorry, sir, but we cannot serve anyone who does not have on a tie and jacket."

Billy stared at him, not understanding and suddenly growing very nervous about this place. He did not know how to get out of it, did not know where he could run to if anything happened.

"Sir, I'm afraid I'll have to ask you to leave."

Billy glanced around at the tables, at the people sitting and eating. He looked carefully at the waiter, at his funny church clothes and rounded, strange-looking face with its huge nose.

"Do you understand, sir?" Something in Billy's face made the waiter think he might not.

Billy looked around the room. Everyone was dressed like they were going to church, and they were all sitting there just eating. There was even some niggers sitting down eating and they were dressed the same way.

"Y'all mean I ain't dressed right?" he asked.

"That's right."

"Is this some kind of church meeting?"

The waiter relaxed and even allowed himself a soft chuckle. "No, this is a restaurant."

Billy looked around the room once more, still not understanding as he watched the people eat, none of them even looking back at him.

He felt the waiter's hand settle on his arm as he turned away toward the window again, but he did not turn back to face him. "Do you leave now, buddy, or do I call the manager?" The waiter's voice was harsh now and Billy could feel the threat in it. He wheeled quickly, grabbing the man's wrist, wrapping his hands around it like a vise, enjoying the surprise and pain that showed in the round face.

And then suddenly he let go and walked away through the dining room, heading back toward the little rooms. If they went up then they must go down too.

20

George was at the reception desk to greet A.L. when he was released from the hospital. He stood there with his bandy legs slightly spread as he watched A.L. being wheeled to the desk where the long wooden crutches waited, propped against the formica edge.

"Hey," George said as the wheelchair drew closer, "how come they letting you go, huh?"

It was part of the way George talked to him, always putting him on, with A.L. coming back with the same kind of put-on.

"They said they was letting me out to go after some Greek who runs a saloon on Main Street East."

"Now who's that, you suppose? Who's that?"

"I don't know, but I'm gonna find him."

A.L. hoisted himself out of the chair, his leg still stiff and sore though the wound was healing now that the drain had been removed. He leaned against the desk and picked up the crutches. They were extra sturdy to support his weight. He snuggled them under his arms, trying to find a comfortable spot.

"Man, I sure ain't gonna like walking on these wood legs."

"Be glad it's not for all time," George said.

A.L. put a little weight on his wounded leg, testing it. He

could feel the pain in the area of the wound, but the leg was stronger than he had thought it would be.

"Now you remember not to walk on that leg for at least two weeks, Mr. Smith," said the nurse at the desk as she looked over the papers in front of her on the clean-topped counter.

"I don't think I could anyway," A.L. said. He stood hunched over because of the crutches.

"Those are the longest crutches we have," the nurse said. "I'm sorry."

"Oh, that's all right."

"Yeah, he just learn to walk shorter," George said.

They walked out together, George ready to help should A.L. need it. A.L. used both legs and only took some of the weight off his right with the crutch on that side.

"This ain't too bad," he said as he swung down the steps. "I think I could learn to walk real easy this way."

"Just don't start no fights, that's all," George said as he opened the door of his car.

They drove along through the heavy traffic on East Avenue, fighting the noontime crush with the car horns bleating like impatient sheep. When they stopped to turn onto the Inner Loop, A.L. looked down at his feet and then back up at George, who was watching the light, waiting for it to change so he could jump it and beat the oncoming traffic turning left in front of them.

"I don't know how to thank you," A.L. said.

"No thanks necessary."

"Well there is, because if it hadn't been for you I was one dead nigger."

"You just get that leg back in shape so you can go to work and we can get started on the houses. I talk with a woman the other day, Mrs. Pile. She say she give us plans for finishing insides of the houses. And she do that for nothing."

"For nothing? Je-sus!"

"What you Jesusing for?"

"I never knew there was so many people would help."

"They around, but you gotta go look for them. Like anything else, they don't come look for you."

They swept around the Inner Loop, heading downtown by the big Public Safety Building and down to Main Street. Once off the loop they hit the traffic lights again and the thick snarl of cars.

"I still don't see how Mr. Morton got me sprung so easy, especially after that story in the paper."

"He told me they was gonna keep you, but when that man got killed after you locked away, they didn't have no choice."

"You mean even with you alibiing for me they wasn't gonna let me go?"

"Yeah, that's what he told me. Even then they was gonna charge you for beating up all them cops, but Craig said they couldn't do it because they got you there with no reason."

"It sure felt fine when he called Tuesday afternoon and told me it looked good. Then, I woke up yesterday and the guards was gone. I couldn't believe it. He's some smart."

"His mother's a Greek," said George.

"Well it don't matter none to me. He got me out and when those goons grabbed me this time I thought I was all done. They ain't never believed the truth before, so I figured I might as well mess them up good as I could before they charged me with whatever it was they had on their mind."

George laughed. "You done a good job on them. That's all anybody talking about except for the murders. What I don't understand is how they just come get you so easy."

"The only thing I can think of is, they just run down everybody they could find that had a record. Then they looked for someone who might have a reason to go around killing whites and maybe got somebody to shoot their mouth about when I was drunk a couple of times and said how I owed certain people some damage."

"Is like Greece."

"I don't know, but I do know that when those goons decide to bust a black they don't worry none about evidence. Tell you what else, too. I ain't out of it yet. I wouldn't be surprised if them clowns come looking for me when they're off duty."

"In Greece that happen all the time. Both my father and me was beaten up four, five times. We was lucky to get away."

"Man, no wonder you don't like cops."

"Cops, soldiers, all the same to me. But no matter. We got better things to do, huh? When we get to my place I got a good lunch for you and later we talk and then sign some of those papers."

"Sure, man. Sooner we get going the better. I'd like to get the outside work done by the end of fall."

21

"I'M GOING for a walk," Daniel said. "Lock the door after me and be sure all the windows are locked."

"Are you going to the police?" Sarah Ann asked.

"I don't know. Just for a walk. I still have to think about it." He stood looking at her as if he had never seen her before. Suddenly he did not understand why she had such a firm hold on him, why she could lead him so with her tears and her voice. It was as if they had been living in the dark, and now with the sudden light everything was different.

"Please, don't cry," he said, his tone childishly pleading. "Please don't make me do something I ain't thought out."

"Daniel, you got to do something! For God's sake, he'll kill us!"

He stood with his hands in his pockets, looking down at her face buried in her hands. He loved her hands, loved the delicate tracery of veins across the backs. He shook his head and turned away, running upstairs two steps at a time. He hadn't wanted to do it this way, to leave her unprotected with only the flimsy doors and windows.

He hefted the small thirty-eight, looking at the places where the bluing was worn off, then stuffed the gun into the waistband of his trousers and dropped the rest of the shells into his jacket pocket. It was four years since he'd hunted anything and he had never hunted a man. But he had the advantage of knowing his quarry better than anyone else because of the stalking games they had played when they were kids hunting each other through the tall piney woods. Daniel looked into the mirror on his dresser and turned quickly away, shutting off the light and heading downstairs to the living room.

"I'm going now," he said.

She looked up at him from where she sat, legs curled under her in the shabby chair, her eyes seeming twice their size because of the tears. "What if he comes here? What can I do?" She dropped her head into her hands, her light silky hair flopping forward.

Daniel dropped down on one knee in front of the chair, wanting to comfort her, to calm her, just because she was upset and afraid and he had to get that off his mind so it wouldn't interfere with his decision.

He stood up and she looked up at him again. "How long will you be?"

"Not long," he said, stopping at the door as she walked over toward him. He kissed her softly on the end of her nose and she tried a smile.

"Lock the door," he said.

He had not walked to the end of the block before he knew he was being followed. He kept on, not turning or even looking back over his shoulder, trying instead to gauge how far back his pursuer was, skulking along in the dense shadows, avoiding the light but still keeping a safe distance.

On the corner, waiting for the light, he glanced casually back over his shoulder down the empty street. He could not see anyone. He walked on, picking up his pace slightly, forcing Billy to move faster and maybe make a mistake. He was ready now and he had something to protect, and he knew he had the advantage of knowing how his cousin moved, how he would come at him with his knife held low, looking for a shot at the belly and suddenly pointing the blade toward the throat while you tried to protect your middle. To cut across to Plymouth Avenue he chose the brightest side street he could, knowing it would slow Billy down and give him a little time.

When he turned onto Plymouth Avenue he was no longer sure he was being followed, and then he wasn't sure he had even been followed at all. There was more traffic here, and it was harder to pick up sounds that were not really sounds but indications of movement. A can clattered close behind him and he jumped and whirled, only to see a dog trying to force his nose into an empty tin. He began walking again, his heart hammering in his chest, his lungs aching from the attempt to control his breathing.

At the end of Plymouth he crossed the big intersection at the loop and walked up the wide stairs and into the police station, following the signs to the front desk. The building smelled cold and barren and the tile floor had just been washed with some kind of disinfectant that made the place smell slightly like the men's rooms at work. The voices of the men at the desk echoed through the two-story foyer. He walked over to the desk and waited for one of the two policemen.

"What can I do for you?" said the short one whose name tag said Riley.

"I want to talk to somebody about those murders," Daniel said.

"So does everybody," Riley said.

"I know who the killer is," Daniel said, his voice low and insistent.

The sergeant came up behind Riley, standing with his thumbs hooked into his wide leather belt. "What's he want?"

"Says he knows who the killer is," Riley said.

"Look, bud, there's about thirty people a day come in here telling us they know who the guy is. One guy thinks it's his neighbor, another his boss, some woman complained the milkman was acting suspiciously the other morning, and one bitch even reported it was her husband."

Daniel stood with his big hands curled over the moulding strip along the front edge of the counter. It came slightly above his waist.

"The killer is my cousin," he said, his blue eyes steady as he stared at the sergeant.

"You from the South?" Riley asked.

"Georgia. My cousin comes from there too. He left late this spring and he ain't been back."

"So what. A lot of people take off," Riley said.

Daniel dropped his hands from the counter and turned toward the doors opposite the ones he had come through. Outside he walked across the broad stone plaza, his hands rolled into fists inside his pockets. It had not occurred to him that the cops wouldn't believe him.

He stood at the top of the steps leading down to the street, looking off toward the downtown area across the river, suddenly aware that he was alone, that Billy wasn't following him, and immediately he began worrying about Sarah and the kids. If he went back he would make it easy for his cousin. It would give Billy the advantage, making it possible for him to pick his time just like a fox stalking a hen house, waiting until he was sure.

Daniel jogged down the steps and angled across the street toward the big auditorium and the river. He stopped again on the bridge, looking out at the river, watching the water tumbling along in the lights from the small park by the auditorium. Above the arched bridge upstream from him he could see the old railroad station and beyond it the tracks leading off through the city. He should go back. He was sure of it. Billy would know he had left and that Sarah was alone. But still he stood there, looking at the old railroad station, slowly becoming aware of it as a place and then a special place, the kind of place that his cousin might even hole up in. It was deserted and he could sleep out the day when it was too dangerous to hunt.

He left the bridge and walked out around the library building, excited now at the thought that Billy might be there, that he might be able to finish it now. As he walked he realized it was the first time he had been downtown when it was dark. There were lots of cars. He turned at the side street, crossing diagonally when the traffic slowed, and then stayed in close to the rail looking for a way down to the level of the old station. In the blue light from the street lamps he could see that the yellowish paint was badly peeled and in places the wood was completely bare. He stopped and leaned both hands against the chill pipe of the bridge railing, letting it cool the sweat on his palms.

Back the way he had come, he saw a ladder down to the station platform. He stopped again when he reached it, waiting now for a lull in the traffic. When it came, he vaulted over and scurried down the ladder. Now on the platform, he moved as quickly as he could, keeping low so he didn't have to stop and check to see what kind of background there was and whether it would silhouette or conceal him.

He kept his back to the wall of the station, holding his breath, listening for any sound. There was only the city breathing at him with the sound of the automobiles on the bridge and the rumble of machinery off in the distance. Up on the bridge he saw a woman rushing along and for an instant he thought it might be Sarah, but he knew she would never have left the children.

He tried to decide which side of the building to check first. Either the back or the river. If Billy had forced one of the heavy shutters it would have to be there, where it would not be easily noticed. Daniel crept around to the long side by the river and moved slowly along, walking on the balls of his feet now, hoping he wouldn't hit a rotten board and go through.

If he hurt a leg he would have to wait for Billy to come to him. About halfway down he froze into the dark, his ear against the building, sure he had heard someone cough inside. He waited but the sound did not come again.

He found the open shutter on the back just around the corner. It was a bad place. Anyone inside would be guarding the one entrance. Billy would just stand inside, so that even if you rushed in he'd be on you from behind, before you could stand up.

Daniel backed off to where there was a drop in the platform to another level four feet lower. He eased over the edge until only his head showed above the weathered beam. It was too big a risk. Billy would already know he was out there and he would be ready. What would Sarah do if he got killed? Go back to Georgia? She couldn't do that and yet she couldn't stay here either, not with his cousin around.

Besides, the cops wouldn't be looking for him until it was too late. His palms were damp with sweat, and without thinking he pulled the gun from his belt before blotting off his hands. He ducked out of sight to wipe off the gun and to dry his hands. If one finger slipped he would miss whatever chance he would have.

There was one chance. The shutters opened in, which meant they had probably taken the windows out. If he came in at an angle and dove as far as he could and came up on his back it would give him enough time. Suddenly he was up on the platform and running as low and fast as he could, taking the window sill in one stride and crashing through into darkness, rolling, turning, aiming the gun back at the window, even as he heard something scramble hard in back of him in the far corner of the big open building. He flopped onto his belly and cut loose two shots, the flashes from the gun nearly blinding him in the almost total dark. He waited, holding his breath until he thought his lungs would burst, and then he heard another sound, a sort of whimper.

"Billy!" he shouted, and his voice echoed hard in the wooden building. "Billy! I'm gonna kill you!"

He waited, but there was no sound. "I got to, Billy, you know that!"

When he moved again Daniel cut loose another round. The bullet, slammed into the thick wooden wall, and the muzzle blast of the gun sounded as loud as a ten-gauge shotgun. He cocked the hammer. "Billy!"

Suddenly there was a flare of light from a match. "Don't shoot! Oh Christ, don't shoot." The voice was creaky. "God, mister, I ain't Billy!"

Daniel walked closer, peering through the dark at the man holding the match beneath his face. He was old and he had several weeks' growth of whiskers. He smelled as if he had never taken a bath in his life, unless maybe to try and wash himself with cheap wine.

Daniel whirled away from him, running through the dark toward the window, leaping through and running down the platform away from the bridge. Somebody had probably heard the shots. He found the ramp and ran on down the tracks and then as he hit the roadbed turned on the speed, running until the only sound he could hear was the rush of his own breathing and his heart so loud it was like being inside a big drum, and still he ran, occasionally stumbling, but catching himself and staggering ahead anyway. He didn't see the loose tie lying across his path, and his foot hit it squarely, pitching him toward the ground. He got his hands up just in time to keep from plowing his face into the sharp cinders and crushed stone.

He lay there with the pain in his lungs like a fire, finally rolling onto his back, waiting for his breathing to slow so he could hear. He tried holding his breath, but it only made his heart sound louder and he still could not hear. It seemed forever before his breathing returned to normal. No one had followed, no sirens were going.

Slowly Daniel pulled himself off the ground. His foot hurt

where he had caught it, but nothing seemed to be broken. It wasn't until he started to brush himself off that he realized he was still carrying the gun. He looked at it, resting in the palm of his hand, hardly able to believe he had come so close to killing that poor old wino. He walked to the water and threw the gun out over the river, watching as it splashed and sank. He was glad to be rid of it.

Down the tracks he could see the bridge that crossed over to the yards on the other side, and he started toward it, walking slowly. It had started to rain softly, a warm rain that felt good. He decided maybe it would be best if he just stopped thinking about his cousin and the murders before he ended up dead himself.

22

BILLY SAT on his rolled-up blanket, looking out through the tunnel entrance at the glow from the city. Everything had changed now and he was itching to leave, to go home to Georgia. The police would find him sooner or later now that Daniel had talked to them. He would have told them where to look. He hated Daniel worse now than he ever had before, and he knew now he would have to kill him.

A breeze danced through the jagged mouth of the tunnel and he could smell the rain, still a couple of hours away. Daniel would know where to look for him, would know what kind of place he would choose. He could not stand the thought of prison. He did not want to be pushed into moving, either, and he was not ready to leave.

But the tunnel was no longer a good place. There was only one way out. At the far end there was a platform and two large doors which were usually locked except when a train was coming with the paper. But then the train was his only way out of the city, except to follow the river south. He wished he were back there now.

When he was nervous Billy sat with his hands folded and his index fingers pressed together, working them back and forth, back and forth, tightening his muscles until it hurt. He tried to relax, to calm himself, but he could not. Every sound rang through the tunnel, echoing back, bouncing back off his nerves, setting him up. He stood up and threw the blanket roll over his shoulder and walked out of the tunnel, not knowing what sort of place he was looking for, but knowing it would have to be nearby so he could watch for a train.

Billy walked along the tracks between the rails, his stride too short to walk every other tie and too long to walk on every tie, and so he moved unevenly, slowly, his feet slipping from the ties onto the stone. He almost passed the little switchman's shed without seeing it. The shed was small, only slightly bigger than the outhouse back home. He walked over to the door and then around to the window on the side. The shed looked empty, but the dark made it hard to see inside.

He broke the lock off the door with a rock, scarring the old, red wood. There was a bench tacked to the wall inside, and he closed the door and sat down. It was bigger than he had thought, but during the daytime anyone passing in a train could easily see inside. His eyes were adjusted to the dark now, and the floor was clear. He stood up, wrapped himself in his blanket and curled up on the floor, well below the window sills.

He heard the rain coming, marching steadily across the city and then drumming on the roof. But even with the steady drone of the rain he could not sleep. It was time to run, and he knew suddenly that it was not just the train he was waiting for but something else.

Billy sat back up on the bench and took out his knife and his small whetstone, spitting on the stone and then working the blade against it, thinking through the contentment the grinding sound always brought. He would have had to leave this place when the leaves fell anyway, so even if Daniel had not told the law it would not have made much difference, except that it was harder to run when there was someone looking for you. There would be no one looking for him if Daniel had not gone to the sheriff.

"Why'd you do that, Daniel?" he asked, his thin voice straining against the dark as the tears ran down his cheeks. "Why, Daniel? I never done nothing to you except when we was kids and even then it was just because we was kids. You made it hard for me, Daniel, you put the law onto me."

He wiped the blade on his trousers and slid it into the sheath. He looked out at the rain and decided to leave his blanket roll in the shed. He tucked it underneath the seat, as far out of sight as he could, and then stepped out into the rain. He put the lock back in place so no one would know he had been there.

Now he headed down the tracks, dog-trotting on the side of the roadbed, moving easily along in the rain, heading south toward Clarissa Street, turning off and up through the empty lots, trotting easily, steadily until he reached the street.

Billy walked boldly out into the open and moved down the rain-soaked street, his hair matted from the rain that washed away the sticky tracks from his tears. He licked his upper lip where the water had collected, tasting the salt.

Even as he came within a block of the house he did not know what he was going to do. His boots were sodden now, and he could hear them squishing as he walked. The street was empty and even as the rain came down harder, splattering heavily on the pavement, Billy could hear his boots talking to him. His clothes were soaked and heavy, and he could not walk as fast. He stopped, standing with his head down, looking at the reflection of a streetlight on the wet sidewalk. He would be too stiff and his clothes too heavy to fight.

He started walking again, and when he reached Daniel's he turned into the vacant house across the street and climbed up to the second floor. He peeled off his clothes and boots, carefully wringing them out and hanging them on nails and hooks to dry. He found a piece of torn curtain still hanging by one of the side windows and tore it off to use as a towel, before curling up to try sleeping. He was too cold and he stood up and paced back and forth in the room, gradually warming from the motion. He walked around the edges next to the walls, moving quickly by the windows, his feet falling softly in the stillness. He should never have left the shed. He was trapped here now and Daniel would know he was being watched. Daniel was a good hunter, all the Hewses were. Close to midnight Billy wrapped himself in the ragged curtain and curled up in the large closet at the back of the room.

The sound of the fence gate across the street awakened him around two A.M. and he crawled over to the window ledge to watch the big nigger on crutches fussing with the catch on the gate. It had stopped raining.

Billy saw him work his way up the narrow sidewalk to the front door, swinging his right leg and using his left. He did not like him being around. He was too tall and too thick and his throat too difficult a target. If he missed and the man got hold of him he would be through.

At the door the man looked up toward Billy's window, but Billy ducked down even before the man's head had fully turned.

When he heard the bang of the screen door he waited several minutes and looked out again. The man was gone. He walked back to the closet and curled up, knowing now what he had to do.

23

DANIEL WAS ONLY a few feet farther on when the rain burst over him in a streaking downpour, soaking him until the weight of his clothes dragged down on him, their heaviness matching his mood. He was just plodding now, and his foot was beginning to throb hard just behind his toes where he had caught it on the tie. He stuffed his big hands into his pockets and hunched his shoulders against the rain, bowing his head. He limped now along the roadbed, trying to stay off the ties so he wouldn't chance coming down on the ball of his injured foot.

The rain did not slacken but kept steadily on, the big drops dashing themselves against the stone and the steel and the creosoted ties.

He could not understand how his imagination had got hold of him so completely, but he understood now that it happened to people, that something you felt guilty about could make you think what wasn't real was real.

He walked along the edge of the roadbed where it was more level and he could at least keep his sore foot on even ground. His heavy black hair was wet and strung out over his forehead and he brushed it back, squeezing some of the water into his eyes.

What if he had killed the old man? It was crazy! If he hadn't had that pack of matches he'd be dead by now. Poor old man, just laying there sleeping it off and somebody starts shooting at him. Daniel realized that probably the cops wouldn't have known who'd done it and they probably wouldn't have cared. But he would have known, and he didn't see how he could have lived with that on his conscience along with Charlie Clay.

The roadbed widened and it was higher, topping a gentle slope to the river bank. He could see across to the far side where the boxcars sat in blocky rows in the yards.

He nearly passed the switchman's shed without seeing it, and he would have walked right on by if it hadn't been for the fresh scar in the old red paint. He stopped and looked at the lock. It was open. Someone must have broken in and then fixed the lock when they left so you wouldn't see it was open unless you looked closely.

Daniel took the look off and opened the door, the hair on the back of his neck prickling, and there was a smell, a familiar smell that he couldn't place. Under the bench he found a blanket and when he unrolled it the smell grew stronger. It was dark and hard to see inside the shack and he took the blanket to the door, but that was no help, the only light coming from across the river and the rain so thick and steady it cut way down on that. He sat down on the bench and took out his cigarettes. The pack was wet, but he found one dry enough to smoke under the end of the pack still covered by the shiny foil.

Here his imagination was, at it again! He was sitting in this old beat-up shed thinking that Billy Oakes had been there and all he had was a blanket that was probably left by some hobo while he went off panhandling. What better place to leave his stuff, right where he could hop a freight without anyone seeing him.

He got up and walked out of the shack, leaving the door swinging open, and then went back and closed it, fixing the lock.

The rain had slowed now and as he walked down the tracks with the bridge in sight up ahead it changed again to a fine drizzle, wispy and wet, as soaking as the downpour had been. He wished he were home and dry and warm.

When he reached the bridge he stopped, pulled the bullets from his pocket, and threw them into the river one by one, waiting for the splash before he threw the next. He stood looking downstream at the peaceful water for a while, then moved on.

The rain had stopped by the time he reached the house, and the air was cool and slightly cleaner somehow. Sarah had moved the chair up against the door, and he stood dripping on the hall floor while she pushed it away.

"Daniel, you're soaked."

He put both his hands on her shoulders and kissed her hard, keeping her away from his sodden clothes, and then just holding her at arm's length, smiling.

"What happened?" she asked, smiling back at him, still hesitantly.

"Nothing happened," he said as he peeled off his jacket. "C'mon upstairs and I'll tell you about it while I get some dry stuff on."

She lay on the bed, her legs crossed at the knees, leaning down onto her elbow as she listened.

"I went to the cops and they treated me like I was crazy. They said all kinds of people come in there every day telling them they know who the killer is. I had the gun with me and I decided to go after Billy. I saw the old railroad station across the river and I found a shutter that was loose, and I figured for sure he was in there hiding in the dark, but come to find out it was just an old bum." He stood naked, toweling himself dry. "What I'm trying to say is, this whole thing has been in my imagination, you know? It don't make sense that Billy would come all the way up here from Georgia. He probably just wandered off into the woods and up into Tennessee somewhere and got himself shot."

It was too quick a shift for her and she sat silent, waiting for him to go on.

He sat down next to her on the bed. "I'm sorry, honey, for getting you all upset about this, but I didn't know before how worried I was about that Charlie Clay thing and not getting Billy put in jail."

She started to cry, and then suddenly folded into his arms. "Oh, God, Daniel, I was so scared. I was so scared. All I could think about was that time when he came into my room back home, and his hands all over me."

He held her tightly, smoothing her dress and then curling his hand around the back of her head and tucking it in against his shoulder as she cried, her body shaking hard with the deep sobs that now were a relief to him because once it was over she would have done the crying for both of them.

Over the sound of her crying he first thought he heard the old dead elm in the back yard scratching against the dry clapboards. Then he waited, listening, still holding Sarah tightly so she wouldn't know. The sound was out of cadence with the soft wind that had come following the rain, and suddenly he knew it was a tool being worked against a window catch. He drew in a breath and held it so he could hear better and now Sarah, feeling his sudden tension, was listening too.

"Daniel, what is it?" The edges of her voice cracked with the fear.

"Another one of those damn junkies," he said.

Slowly he got up off the bed and crept out of the room and down the stairs, setting each foot before taking the weight off his back foot. The sound was from the kitchen window. Christ, he wished he still had the gun. He could have just fired right on through the drawn shade and the window. It would not have been possible to miss.

He slipped into the kitchen and over to the stove, picking the heavy iron skillet off the cold burner, waiting now for whoever it was to get the window up enough to give him a clear shot. It seemed like an hour before the window began to slide up. He had to wait and time it so the man's head would be just inside and then throw the pan as hard as he could.

The window stopped moving and suddenly a light clicked on in the house next door and Daniel could see him silhouetted perfectly against the shade and he threw the pan. It was a perfect shot, only the man had moved, ducking the light, and the pan caught him on the arm as he was turning. He yelled once and as Daniel heard him running off, he dashed over to where the pan had torn the shade away, hanging out to see if he could spot him.

The pan lay upside down on the floor of the alley, and the shade flapped against the side of the house in the wind. The man was gone.

He walked back across the kitchen to the living room shaking his head, fighting the belief that it had been his cousin. He opened the front door for a moment and stared hard at the vacant house across the street.

"Daniel?"

"Huh?"

"You all right?" Sarah had no color at all in her face.

He shut the door with a slam. "Uh-huh. Just some junkie, like I said."

24

BILLY WAS WATCHING the next morning when the big nigger came out of the house and hobbled down the walk, noticing which leg was injured and how he used the light brown sticks to support his weight as he worked his way down the street. He watched him until he turned out of sight around the corner of a squat building, the bricks red in the morning sun that was making kettles of steam out of the puddles from last night's rain.

Now Daniel came out of the house carrying a shiny metal box. He stopped at the gate, leaning back against the fence, the metal mesh sagging slightly as he rested between two posts. He lit a cigarette, cupping his hands against a sudden breeze, and then flipped the match out into the street where it landed between two puddles. As he smoked he occasionally glanced down the street. A car pulled up and stopped and Daniel walked over and opened the door and climbed into the back where Billy could see two other men. He could hear their voices, but he could not make out what they were saying. The car moved a few feet and then suddenly stopped and Daniel jumped out and ran into the house and came back out almost immediately, trotting toward the car, stopping at the door and looking around before he climbed in. He knew he was being watched, Billy decided. That was good. Complete surprise was better, but Daniel would be waiting, knowing he was coming but not knowing when. Picking the time to move would give Billy the advantage. He would need it with Daniel because of his size. He was nearly as wide as that big black man on the sticks, though nowhere near as tall.

By noon his clothes were dry and he put them on, returning as soon as he could to his window.

The sun had swung around and was pouring through the window now, and it made him drowsy. He had waited for Sarah Ann to leave but she had not and he decided to let himself sleep.

The slam of a car door woke him and he carefully peeked around the edge of the window frame. It was the police, two of them standing by their car talking and looking at the house. He would be cornered here if they came in, and he could not run now because they would be sure to see him. The only way was up. He heard a door squeak downstairs as he climbed into the attic, looking for another way out.

The window in the north end was only two feet or so from the wall of the brick building next door. He opened the window and stepped out, climbing onto the ledge and then, using his hands and legs to wedge himself into the slot, began working his way up toward the roof of the next building.

The rain had soaked the walls and the bricks were still slippery. Twice he nearly fell, and only the strength he drew out of his fear held him like a fly to the sides of the buildings.

The cops were in the attic now and he had only two feet to climb. Slowly he inched his way up, his fingers raw from the sharp edges of the bricks and crumbling concrete. He grabbed the edge above him with one hand and then, reaching back for an extra bit of strength, hooked his other hand over and slowly pulled himself to the top, just getting a knee up. The cops were closer now, and Billy rolled himself over the wall without looking down and then suddenly clawed back at the edge, catching it with one hand as he dangled some twenty feet above the charred timbers of the burned-out building. He could hear them talking as tiny crumbs of mortar rained by him, clattering into the dark hole.

"Nothing out here, Harry," one of them called, and Billy realized the man was just below him, the wall between.

"I wish to hell those renewal people would knock these things down. I'm sick of having to check them all the time," the other man said.

He waited, trying to hold his body still to relieve as much as possible the strain on his fingers, clutching the cement cap on top of the wall. His muscles cramped with the strain and his stomach was pushed hard against his backbone but still he hung there, his feet dangling free, not daring to move before he heard the car doors close. If he climbed back up too soon they would be able to see him from the street. He looked both ways. Toward the back of the ruined building there were the butts of several broken rafters protruding from the brick wall, and he decided to work himself that way, hoping they were high enough to rest his feet and take the weight off his hands. He moved one hand, and then the other, his chest brushing against the smoke-blackened wall, the soot coming off on his coat and his face as he swung against the wall. He wished he had never come to this place and he hated Daniel more than ever. He tried to relieve the pressure on his hands by searching in the crevices of the wall for toeholds, but he could find none and he wasted time trying.

Now he hung, swaying slowly, alternating his weight from hand to hand as he worked along the wall. And then the rafter ends were beneath his feet and he could reach them with his toes just enough to take some of the pressure off his hands. He worked along toward an area where parts of the top floor remained, testing each broken rafter carefully, holding the edge of the wall above him with his hands and trying to look down over his shoulder to see what he was standing on. Finally he was over the section of floor. It was a good eight-foot drop and it might not hold, but the muscles in his hands were cramping badly. He heard the car drive off and out front just as he let go and dropped onto the charred flooring, the boards giving way beneath him and dropping him in a clattering shower onto the next floor. It held—he had landed well.

He had never been so exhausted. He sat rubbing his hands, trying not to fall asleep, but knowing that he would because he always slept after coming so close to being killed. It was almost dark when he awoke, and he sat up rubbing his eyes and then his bruised hands, kneading them carefully to loosen the muscles in his fingers and forearms. In the gloom the hate and anger seeped out of his blue eyes, sparkling in the small shafts of light that leaked in through the cracked walls and the windows below. His shoulder was sore and stiff where he had been hit with the pan, but he did not think the effort of hanging from the wall had hurt it any more.

25

DANIEL THREW OPEN the door of the old Nash and stormed around to the front, fiddling with the rusted hood latch. Goddamn the fucking thing anyway. It never worked right, never wanted to start until he'd spent a half-hour or so pleading with the goddamn thing. He pinched his finger in the latch.

"You bastard!" he shouted. "You bitch!" He hauled off and kicked the bumper. The shock released the hood latch and with a wrenching squeak it slowly opened.

Daniel peered in, still holding his hand. He was not a mechanic but he had managed to learn about things like plugs and points.

He walked around and climbed in again, trying the starter and listening to it grind and grind, not showing even a spark of life. He shut off the key and went around to the front again, looking down at the dirty, grease-encrusted engine. At least the battery wasn't dead this time. He raked his fingers through his hair, scratching softly with all five fingers, almost massaging his head. He couldn't decide whether the thing was not getting gas or not getting a spark.

The back door banged and Sarah came out to see whether the car was acting up or not. From the way Daniel's eyes were tight at the corners she knew enough not to ask, and she just stood there waiting to see what would happen.

He reached in and checked all the spark plug wires and then pulled the distributor cap off and looked at the points, working them once to make sure they weren't stuck.

The engine ground and ground and once nearly caught. When it missed, he turned the key off again.

"What's wrong with it?" asked Sarah. Her confidence in her husband did not extend to cars.

"Must be the fuel line."

"What's that? Is it serious?"

"Look, Sarah, how in hell am I gonna fix this thing if you're gonna stand here asking me all kinds of questions?"

"I'm sorry," she said.

He pulled two wrenches from the box of tools he kept in the trunk and began removing the fuel filter. He had it nearly off when Sarah asked, "Daniel, do you really think it was all in your imagination?"

"Uh-huh."

"The police wouldn't even listen to you?"

"They acted like I was a nut of some kind."

He pulled himself out from under the hood, holding the fuel filter in his hand. "I think that's the trouble all right," he said. "See where all that dirt has clogged it up?"

"Uh-huh," she said.

He picked an empty beer can up off the ground and leaned over the engine. "Go turn it over," he said.

"How?"

"Just turn the key all the way over until I tell you to stop."

The sound of the engine startled her, but she held the key over until he shouted.

He was sitting on the ground pouring gas from the beer can over the fuel filter as she walked around front.

"Do you think it will work now?"

"Ought to," he said.

She stood quietly watching him, wondering what she would tell the children if he couldn't get the car going and there was no picnic. "Daniel, when are we going to move out of this horrible old place?"

"Soon as I can get the money. Do you know what other places cost?"

"No," she said.

"Well, for a family our size, about twice what we pay here."

"That much?"

"Uh-huh." He blew on the ends of the filter where the lines connected. "You know, it was funny when I was inside that old station last night. I could have sworn Billy was there or at least that he had been there."

She ignored the comment. "You gonna ride to work every day with those same men now?"

"I think so, but it'll mean I have to use my car once in a while to make it fair." He held the filter up and looked it over carefully. "Did that woman come again today?"

"Which woman?"

"The one about the reading."

"No. She comes tomorrow."

He leaned in over the engine, carefully reinstalling the filter, humming to himself as he worked. "Okay," he said, "that oughta do it."

He walked around and turned on the key. The engine ground and coughed and ground and then started. He revved it a few times and left it running as he came around to close the hood.

"It works?" she said.

"Of course it works."

"I guess you're the smartest husband in Lakeport," she said, coming up on her toes to kiss his cheek.

Daniel smiled and held her close, not even glancing at the house across the street.

26

HE HATED THE CRUTCHES, not just because they slowed him up but because all his life he had depended on his body more than anything else. It was what had gotten him through the worst times. He had always been able to count on it, even in the pen where it helped keep people off your back until you had time to think things out. You either got smart there or you didn't make it.

There were the quiet, little men who would just as soon kill you as look at you, and there were the ones who were never involved in any of the action but were always around to benefit from whatever happened while you spent time in the hole.

The crutches left him at the mercy of the cops. They could come up on him before he even had a chance to react and set himself. And then he would have to protect his leg, putting him on the defensive. The only thing to do was just what he was doing, staying loose, not settling in one place too long. You never saw a hurt dog move into a fight. Keeping moving would make it hard for them to pin him long enough in one place where it was safe for them to come in on him. He'd spend a couple of hours at his apartment and then head for George's. Some nights he'd find a chick to stay with.

He hobbled along, the sound of the crutches echoing against the hollow buildings. Sweating hard from the effort, he was surprised at how far out of shape he was.

"It's all that damn fat, man, that's what it is. You lugging around twenty-five pounds of stomach from all that beer and potatoes and you are just plain fat. Shit, them motherfucking cops come after your ass now, they'll fuck you over before you can even take a damn breath."

He didn't like walking alone on the street. As long as there were other blacks around, the cops would have to be more careful. It wasn't like the old days so much now. They couldn't bust you quite so easy and there was no way they could beat you up on the street and get away with it. Of course you still couldn't be sure they wouldn't try.

He turned and walked away from Clarissa Street, up toward where there were more lights and more people. If the buses were still running he could catch one and get over to George's. It was almost shorter to walk because you went in a straighter line, but his leg was beginning to hurt and he just didn't want to spend that much time alone in dark, secluded places. Not only were there the cops to worry about, there was still that killer running loose. At least he hadn't killed any blacks yet.

A.L. grinned as he realized just what he was doing. He had never run from anything before, not ever. The funny thing was, it didn't seem to bother him. It wasn't like he had a choice.

The red newspaper truck was just pulling away after leaving some papers for the machine when A.L. reached the corner. That meant it had to be about ten-thirty. The Circle Market was closed, but the drugstore up in the next block was open and he could see the red neon sign in front of the Odd Fellows, flashing on and off, off and on. For a club they usually had good music, and he wondered who was playing there now. The main thing was, he just didn't feel like going all the way downtown.

There was a middle-of-the-week crowd in the Odd Fellows

Hall. He nodded to a couple coming out as he waited to pay his dollar to old Pete Fields. About all Pete was good for was sitting on his worn stool, taking a dollar from each customer. He had been that way ever since his wife was killed in a fire. But once, somewhere back in his past, he had been a fight fan and he knew A.L. and would honor him with a feint and a quick toying left lead, a soft swing that A.L. always let glide by his chin. Then Pete would grin and say, "Hey, baby, when's your next fight?"

A.L. sat on the long front side of the bar, near the middle where he could still see the small stage but well away from the door. He ordered a shot and a beer, popped the shot fast, and then settled into drinking the beer. He liked the way it sozzled his mouth, tracking down every trace of the slightly acid bourbon, leaving just the warmth.

Down at the end of the place, off to his left, there was a Panther cat and a couple of chicks and off to the right there was a black dick. He was tall, as tall as A.L., only thin and mean-looking. A.L. wondered which way the cat would jump if Kelly came down looking for him. He sipped at the beer, looked into the glass, and then drained it. Probably go with Kelly.

"Hey, Eddie, gimme another," A.L. said.

"Same?"

"Yeah."

The musicians were coming up onto the small stage behind the cop. He had never heard of them before and he thought now, watching them, that maybe he should have heard of them because they looked like they had been around awhile. They all had shades on and naturals and goatees. The sax man had on one of those African shirts. He didn't know what they were called, but he liked the way they just sort of hung. They looked a whole lot better than the suit the cop was wearing.

The music was very, very easy. He did not know much about it other than that it was some kind of jazz, but it was easy and just what he had wanted to find here on a Wednesday night. It made him feel very cool and he drained his beer glass. Eddie poured a third round without being asked.

He wondered if he ought to go see George. They had a lot to talk about if they were going to get started before the end of summer. He wanted to get all the wiring and all the outside work done so he could move inside once the weather turned. He figured he could have at least one of the houses ready by Christmas. If he could find enough people to work weekends without getting paid right away, he could do both of them. But with just him and the kid they'd get one done for sure. Maybe the thing to do was to get men who worked in the trades and were looking for a good place to live to trade their work for six months' rent. If he had four families and two of them were in the building, the income from the other two would pay off the loan and the taxes and maybe even the insurance.

He decided that the time to see George was in the morning. He wasn't so busy mornings and they could sit down in the back and have a cup of coffee and discuss the whole thing. Anyway, his leg was hurting and he didn't want to go all the way over there even if he could take the bus part way.

With his elbows rested on the mahogany edge of the bar he held the shot glass between the palms of his hands, rolling it slowly without spilling a drop of the amber whiskey. He didn't have to look around to know the cop was watching him. He tossed off the shot and chased it quickly with a swallow of beer and when he looked back down out of the corner of his eye he could see the cop moving around the end of the bar and coming up on him. There wasn't anything to do but wait.

"You Smith?" the cop asked as he leaned in against the bar between the stools.

"You know who I am."

The cop shook his head. "Listen, baby," he said, "you better get it together about me."

"What you mean?"

"I come over here to talk to you as a black man, not a cop, you understand?"

"I'm listening."

"Okay, man. Look, I don't blame you for feeling like you been fucked over, but you ought to know that you done a lot of people a big favor. On account of what you done there's a shake-up going on. Two guys been suspended already and the Chief got a reprimand from the Public Safety Commissioner. What's more, the newspaper got caught because they believed the Chief and they are after his head."

A.L. looked around at the thin hawk face. It was hard, a face as tough as some of those he'd seen in the pen. There was only one way you got that kind of look. "You jivin' me, man?"

"Why would I?"

"You a cop, ain't you?"

"That's right."

"So how I know you ain't setting me up?"

The cop smiled a thin, dangerous smile that drew his lips away from the two rows of slightly yellowed teeth. Slowly the smile changed, without the face changing, just draining the irony out of his eyes. "On account of those two guys getting suspended," he repeated. "On account of that I got promoted to lieutenant."

"Well, ain't that something!" A.L. shook his head, turning fully around on the stool to face the cop. "I been scared half to death to even go outside, afraid they'd come after me again, you know, set me up, plant a knife and say they caught me in the act."

"They might have if they wasn't being watched so close. And I told you about the paper. You remember the reporter that was there the night you got shot?"

A.L. looked right at him, his eyes going blank with the effort of trying to remember. "Hey," he said. "The white cat with the mustache."

"Yeah, that's him. If he hadn't been there they probably

would've killed you. He didn't like what he saw, and he figured out what was going on and he let them know he had figured it out. Shit, man, they can't do nothing. I thought maybe that reporter might be a friend of yours."

"Never saw him before."

"Well he's a good friend of a friend of yours. George."

"From the saloon?"

"Yeah."

"You sure know a lot about me."

The cop shrugged. "Well, man, you were a suspect and it was my job to check you out."

"You tell them to bust me?"

The cop grinned. "My report was on the Public Safety Commissioner's desk when they busted you. It said there was no grounds for arresting you. Shit hit the fan when the Commissioner came in next day. He didn't know nothing about it until he saw the paper in the morning."

A.L. hadn't felt so good in years.

"I'll tell you something else you don't know, and that's who your friends are. You notice that Panther cat when you came in?"

"Yeah, I seen him."

"They know all about you, man, and so do all the brothers and sisters working for RACE. Trouble with you is, you don't know your own people."

"What the hell they care about me? What'd I ever do that they'd notice?"

"You kept your nose clean, you holding down a good job, and when the cops come down on you, you didn't take it, you just busted the heads of the worst racist bastards on the force. Shit, man, you're practically a hero to some people and you don't even know it."

"Well, ain't that something."

"By the way, you need some help with those houses, go see George Hartford over to RACE. He can fix you up."

"How in hell you know about the houses?"

The cop shrugged, but smiling this time, pleased with himself for his thoroughness.

"Man," A.L. said, "this is something. I come in here tonight thinking my string is running out and all of a sudden I got the whole ball back."

The cop stood up, straightening his coat.

"Hey, can I buy you a drink?" said A.L.

"No thanks. Some other time. I'm on duty."

He moved off and A.L. redirected his attention to the music. The band was into some way-out stuff. Usually he liked his sounds more solid, but today it sounded good to him. He was aware that the cop could still be setting him up, that it would be a very good way to get him to let his guard down long enough so they could get him, but he didn't think that was it. What the cop said made sense. And he was right too about his ignoring his own people. Maybe he just hadn't believed they could be any help. They never had before, even when he was in trouble that wouldn't quit. He could feel the old mess boiling up inside him again, though he wanted nothing so much as to believe what the cop had said. It had been a long time since he had many friends. Just George was all. Besides, prison made you a loner. It was the only way you got through without getting stabbed by some queer.

He smiled as he thought about his being a hero. He had been a hero once before, when he was fighting. It was kind of like suddenly finding something you liked a lot that had been lost a long time.

"Hey, Eddie? Gimme another round, huh?"

27

WHEN HE WOKE, Billy eased himself up off the floor, hoisting his body up to the window sill, checking to see how dark it was. The lights were still on in Daniel's house, the yellow paths pushing across the yard, making the discarded bottles and broken glass glow as if they had a light of their own.

It had been stupid to run. He rubbed his left arm where the frying pan had caught him just above the elbow. There was a large black bruise and it was very sore, but there were no bones broken. He needed another way to get inside Daniel's house, some way that would make less noise. If that light hadn't gone on, he might have made it. That was what made this place so dangerous. He could never be sure some other person wouldn't suddenly do something he hadn't expected. There were just too many different things going on all at once, and he did not like having to trust so much to luck.

He slumped down against the rough laths where the plaster had peeled off the wall. Then he leaned forward and pulled the knife from the sheath between his shoulder blades and took the small stone from his pocket and began grinding the blade, carefully maintaining the bite angle.

He might wait until everyone was gone, and then he could take his time and not have to worry about being heard. But he could not remember having seen Sarah Ann leave, not even once. He wished now that he had taken the time to check the window around back before deciding on the side window. The more he thought about it, the more dangerous it seemed. And he realized now that he still did not know whether they were all on one floor or whether they had the first two floors and the big nigger had the third.

Without knowing that, he would have to move very fast and hope there was enough light so he didn't trip over something. If Daniel caught him by surprise he would kill him before he could use his knife. He remembered watching Daniel lift the back end of a wagon out of a ditch, and he was afraid of that strength. He would have to come from behind and get his throat. It was the only way.

The grating sound of the metal and stone seemed loud in the stillness of the deserted house. Billy stopped and looked up over the window ledge, just turning his head enough to see out of the corner of his eye. The lights were still on and he went back to grinding his knife, working it first to a rough wire edge and then honing it smooth with long, sliding strokes of the stone.

He would have to kill them all. That was the only way, catch them by surprise and then Daniel would have to back off to protect his family. That was why his father had slept in the woodshed or the barn. If there was trouble he would only have to defend himself. And if anyone attacked the house they would not expect him from behind.

The sound of the stone made him think again of the warm, wet summers in the hills. He had a favorite place, high up on East Creek where he could sit back under the ledge and see the trail clearly in spite of the heavy underbrush. He remembered watching a big man once, working his way up the trail. He had been fishing and Billy just sat watching, growing more and more curious until he dropped down off the ledge and moved to a spot along the creek where he could get a closer look. Suddenly the two of them were staring right at each other and the man jumped back, frightened by the face hanging in the brush. Billy had simply let go of the bushes he had pried apart, and eased off into the woods. The man was gone by the time he got back up to the ledge. It was the only time he had seen anyone that far up the creek.

He spat on his wrist, exposed below the turned-up cuffs of his jacket, smoothed the hair and shaved a spot clean with a gentle stroke of the knife. Then he put it away, slipping it down into the sheath and leaning back against the broken, crumbling wall. He felt warm inside and he knew the feeling would grow.

He pulled the jacket collar up around his neck and squeezed his arms in against his rib cage, tucking his hands into the armpits, his fingers clutching his sides. He should never have come. It was wrong. The time was wrong. This place alone could kill him. There were not enough hides to run to and the steady noise covered too many other sounds. There was the constant risk of someone coming up behind and—he jumped up, whipping his knife free in one smooth flash of movement, then dropping into a crouch. Now he drifted over the debris and litter on the floor, without a sound, just a fast dark shadow. He stopped at the door and pasted himself against the wall, but he could hear nothing. He held his breath, picking off each sound, trying to find the one that had triggered his alarm. But he could recognize each one and so he put the knife away, letting out a long slow breath, squeezing himself harder and harder against the heat of his anger that made the blood pound at his temples like a drum. Daniel was the one. Daniel had started this, and once he killed Daniel he could go back to Georgia.

He jerked his arms to his sides, and his clenched fists grew white with the strain of keeping them there. Finally the fear began to pass, and his breathing slowed until it was even and regular again.

He crossed to the window. Daniel's lights were out and now

he moved fast, back out the door to the room and down the stairs, coming down on the balls of his feet as soundlessly as a stalking fox. He held still for an instant at the back door before moving on, slipping over the edge of the porch and into the dark alley. Now he walked with extreme care. Anything, a foot coming down on something loose, a startled rat, anything could give him away.

Out on the street not a single car passed and for the first time the city seemed quiet. Billy fought back the growing heat inside, knowing that he could not let it drive him, that he would have to hold it back until he was ready and then go all at once.

He stopped at the end of the alley, looking carefully each way, his eyes prying details out of the dark and checking each movement against the direction and strength of the wind. There was nothing, and he stepped out onto the sidewalk, trying to walk the way he had seen people walk when they didn't have anywhere to go. It was a chance, but he could see no other way. He had to get to the spot between streetlights before he dared cross. Even when he reached the point where the light played out into half-shadowed overlaps, he hesitated, giving the other side of the street a fast check and then walking casually across and turning back toward the house. He remembered that the gate squeaked, that the latch was hard to work, or at least he thought it was from having watched that big nigger struggle with it.

A hundred feet from the house he began angling in toward the corner where the fence and the house were joined together. At that point he suddenly ducked low, moving in a crouched run along the side of the building. There was a light on in the house next door and he turned and moved quickly back up the alley. He moved easily over the low fence and across the front of the building toward the door. He slipped up onto the small porch, moving without caution now, his concentration aiming him like a big cat picking out the one weak animal in the herd.

He wound the door knob slowly, pushing gently even as he turned it, then stopped as he heard a car coming down the street. It was going fast and the headlights would pin him against the house. He eased back on the handle and crouched low, deciding to stay, but a noise inside changed his mind and he bolted, crossing the small yard in three quick strides and taking the fence in a smooth leap.

The driver saw him coming and swerved even as Billy swerved, the car just brushing him. He spun around but managed to keep his balance, then came out of it running, disappearing down the alley in seconds. He wanted distance. Having made the tracks, he turned onto the roadbed and began to slow, finally just dog-trotting along toward the line shack. It would be a good place to sit until he figured out what to do next.

He opened the door and fell onto the bench. He was alone. Off toward Daniel's he heard the screech of car tires and the sound of an engine revving down the street. Suddenly he got up and walked out of the shack, heading back toward the old house. It would be light in six or seven hours and he had to have the dark.

He walked slowly, not wanting to spend too much time by the window because he would get too anxious and move before he was ready again. Back home the coons would be getting fat now and if he were still there maybe he could have just gone on over the mountains into Tennessee and built himself a little cabin and stayed there. With his dogs and knowing the woods he would not have to worry about his backtrail the way he did here. Walking in the city was like being in a strange swamp where each step had to be placed gingerly to make sure you didn't get into a suck hole.

28

JUST AFTER MIDNIGHT Billy decided to go. Now he wasted no time in caution, heading quickly across the street and down the alley. It was the only choice because for the first time there was a light on behind the door in front. The catch had not been fixed, and he eased the window up and then waited, listening for any sounds from inside. There were none and he reached up, grabbing the ledge, and then with a sharp lurch hauled himself up and over and inside. He waited again, crouched below the window, letting his eyes adjust to the darkness.

He slipped his knife free. His eyes were beginning to adjust and he could make out the shape and location of things. It was much brighter in the next room because of the streetlight. He figured from the silence there must be a loft. He could not make out any stairs, and he decided to try the front room. If nothing else he could make sure the door there was open. That would give him another way out besides the side window. The window was a risk. If he had to go fast, he might have to go head-first there and in the dark he could hurt a leg when he landed.

He eased into the living room, trying to stay as close to the walls as possible, where the boards were less likely to squeak. He moved very slowly, taking a step, holding, then taking another. He had to come from behind to get at Daniel and he knew he was doing it wrong, that he should be lying in wait somewhere. But he did not think it was possible to take a man by surprise when you were going after him. That would be especially true of Daniel. He had been raised in the woods and was almost as good a tracker as Billy. But there was a weak spot. Daniel did not kill easily, and he would hesitate even when he had the advantage. It would give Billy a second chance and he could not overlook the possibility of needing one. This was not his place, and Daniel would know where things were even in the dark.

Now Billy moved out into the room, skirting two small chairs and a table and carefully stepping over an object in the middle of the floor. It looked like some kind of toy. He was surprised at the amount of light that came from the streetlight. In the house across the street it had not seemed so bright. At the door he worked the lower bolt and then the turn latch, rotating it slowly to avoid any sharp sound of metal on metal. The upper bolt stuck halfway. He pulled a little harder, but he didn't dare put too much pressure on it. If it went all at once it would sound like gunshot when it hit the stop. The bolts were big, as thick as his thumb, and he wondered what Daniel had to protect that he needed so many bolts.

Billy reached back over his shoulder and slid the knife into the sheath. Then he leaned all his weight against the door, taking the pressure off as he tried the bolt again. This time it slid clear without making a sound. Still he waited before taking his weight off the door.

And now he could feel his own body heat, growing fast, and he wanted to run. Suddenly he knew that he should forget about Daniel and run, just get out, and now the hackles on his neck were alive and he yanked his knife free, crouching and turning, searching for the cause, all his senses tuned.

He picked up the smell of another person, sharp and clear, and at the second he caught it, above and to his left he heard the soft groan of a floorboard at the top of the stairs. He whirled, his knife ready. The place to be was over along the edge of the stairs where he could wait until Daniel had gone by and then move. But he did not dare to cross the room and instead backed off toward the chair in the far corner, slipping down behind it as the lights came on.

"Daniel?" It was Sarah Ann.

"Uh-huh." Daniel stopped about two steps from the top.

"They're in the green bottle on the first shelf."

"Okay."

Billy held himself huddled behind the chair. It was a bad place to be caught. Daniel could use the chair to trap him in the corner. He was sure to notice the window in the kitchen and then the door. Maybe he would think someone had come in and gone, but if he didn't then he would look around. Billy pulled himself in closer, listening as Daniel crossed the room and snapped on the light in the kitchen. A door opened and closed, the light went off, and Daniel started back through the living room.

Halfway across he noticed the bolts on the door and suddenly he knew what had been out of order in the kitchen. The window. He turned quickly and went back to the kitchen, reaching around the corner and yanking the big bread knife from the block by the stove. Whoever it was had either got what he wanted and left or he was still there in the living room. He set the pill bottle on an end table as he scanned the room, inching slowly toward the stairs, knowing he had to protect Sarah and the kids first, that if whoever it was got upstairs he might not be able to get at him.

Outside the front gate squeaked, but if he picked up on it, he did not show any sign. There were chills racing all over him, making every single hair stand up, and his muscles ached from the tenseness that flashed through him.

At the foot of the stairs he stopped, again scanning the room, seeing nothing out of order, nothing missing. He turned his head to look up the stairs and then whirled back around to face whatever it was that had made the tiny noise behind him.

Only Daniel's quick reaction to the sound saved him, and now he held Billy trapped by his eyes in the center of the room, his knife low, the long up-thrust end gleaming. Daniel settled into a crouch, his arms held wide to the sides and the bread knife held upside down so the cutting edge was up to slash.

Neither wanted to make the first move. They stood facing each other as if they had been frozen in stone. Only their eyes moved, duplicating a game they had played as kids, trying to fake the other into anticipating a false move and then darting in to take advantage of the off-balance situation. But that had been a child's game and there had been a willingness to gamble. Now there could be no gamble. Without the surprise, the advantage was Daniel's. He could afford to wait and counter.

Slowly Billy began to circle and it was as if he were performing some kind of ritual dance. His movements were perfect, his body seeming to flow in following each new step.

"Daniel?" Sarah called from the top of the stairs. He reacted immediately, faking with his eyes toward the stairs and Billy came at him, knowing even as he lunged that it had been a fake. Daniel pivoted away on his right foot, spinning away from the knife and slashing up with his own.

But Billy was too quick and he managed to change direction again, sliding out of the way, nearly rolling over in the air as he twisted off and around. He had forgotten about the toy and in turning his foot came down on it, throwing him off balance. He fell backward and slightly to the right and into an end table, sending both the table and lamp crashing against the wall.

"Daniel? Was that you?"

"Stay up there!" he shouted. The talking had cost him his advantage and now Billy was on his feet again and his lips were drawn back and straight and his eyes cold and flat like a cat's.

Steadily he moved in, suddenly looking very sure, circling, trying to make Daniel give up the stairs. But Daniel knew, and in backing away he kept the stairs behind him and the door to his right. He started to talk, hoping to create some kind of distraction that would break Billy's rhythm.

"You'll never get home, Billy," he said. "You'll never see Georgia again. You're gonna rot in prison just like your daddy, boy. Even if you get out you can't get away. You're—"

The door opened so slowly it was as if the wind had pushed it, except that standing there, filling nearly the whole frame of the door, was A.L. Smith. He started talking before the door had swung all the way. "You all right Mr. Hews? I heard—hey what the hell!" He recoiled as the door suddenly opened all the way and he faced Billy.

"Who the hell are you? What you doing with that knife?"

"He's my cousin, Smith. He's the stabber," Daniel said, never taking his eyes off Billy.

"You all right?"

"Yeah."

A.L. shifted his weight onto his good leg and swung one crutch free to fend with. If he could keep the knife away he could use his hands, and he wanted the chance. You didn't get them like this but maybe once in a lifetime. It would be the clincher for him. As he readied himself he tried to remember the time in the pen when he had faced some sawed-off shit with a knife.

"You can't get away, Billy," Daniel said, holding his voice calm and even. "I closed the window in the kitchen and locked it. There's no way out."

Billy stood, held by Daniel's voice. They were both too big. Even a perfect hit would only slow them and if he went for one the other would be on him. He thought about trying the buck. He didn't have a knife and he had a bad leg, but he had those sticks and Billy could see in his eyes that he was more dangerous than Daniel. He would have to have a gun to stop that size. Suddenly he moved, flashing toward the front window, hitting the couch with one foot and hurling himself through the wide pane of glass in the bottom section of the window, balling up to keep from getting cut and rolling even as he hit the ground outside. He never slowed, but came up onto his feet and because of his speed it was hard in the dark to even tell what he was.

He headed for the railroad, hoping there was a train. It no longer mattered about Daniel. He had to get away, get back home, and it had to be now. He flew down across the field faster than he had run it before, dodging the holes and ignoring the risk of falling or stepping on something and twisting an ankle. He just ran.

Even from the top of the field he could see a train pulling slowly along the main tracks, and he adjusted his angle for an open boxcar, picking the spot where he and the car would come together.

He had to go at full speed because even though the train was crawling he would just about make it before the bridge. He could hear only the rush of wind by his ears, and it wasn't until he hit the foot of the embankment that he could hear the clacking wheels of the train and then he was headed up toward the open door of the car, making the steep embankment as if it were flat. He hurled himself into the air at the last possible second and rolled on through the open door, hitting the floor of the car so hard it stunned him. Outside he could hear someone shouting, and he shook his head and scrambled to his feet ready to run again. He was sure from the shouting that he had been spotted. The door on the other side of the car was open, and he crouched in the dark away from the doors, waiting, his knife drawn.

29

A.L. STOOD LEANING on his crutches. "I never saw a man move so fast. He'd have got one of us for sure."

Daniel just shook his head as he looked down at the long knife, remembering how close he had come to striking Billy with it.

"I figured he was fast," A.L. said, "but he surprised the hell out of me when he went for that window."

"Everything about Billy Oakes is a surprise."

"That's his name?"

"Uh-huh." Daniel walked over and set the knife on the end table, then dropped onto the couch, sliding down until the back of his neck rested against the top edge.

"Where'd he learn to use that knife?"

"His father." Daniel looked up quickly. "Sure is a good thing you showed up when you did. I nearly had him once, but I lost the chance and he had me backing down when you came in. All I could think about was my wife and the kids and what he might do if he got upstairs."

"You sure he won't come back?"

"No, not this time. He's scared now and he'll hole up for a day or so and then he'll head back home."

"You ought to call the cops."

"No point in it now. They'd never find him and if they made a lot of noise looking, they might just flush him out and then he'd be sure to kill someone else."

A.L. nodded at the apparent logic, though he knew he would have called the cops. If nothing else they'd be watching here, and he didn't have Daniel's faith that Billy wouldn't come back. After all, he could just walk right out onto the street, and with his blond hair and looking so young nobody would pay him much attention.

"Can't thank you enough for opening that door," Daniel said. "I got so used to not depending on anyone here . . . down home there was always a neighbor."

A.L. studied him carefully, trying to fit the meaning of his words with the southern accent. His instinct was to trust him, but what he was saying might just be a reaction now to what had happened, forgotten tomorrow. If that was true, anything he said now would just make him look foolish. "I might not have tried the door," he said, "but I just had the feeling, you know, that something wasn't right."

"Sure am glad you did."

"You really ain't gonna go to the police tomorrow?"

"I don't know. I went once before and tried to tell them it was my cousin, but they just laughed at me."

"I'll go down with you. There's a black detective who'll listen. They oughta be told, so they don't bust some innocent bastard like me again."

Daniel nodded. "What time?"

"First thing in the morning, say eight or so. I'll get hold of the guy I know and have him there."

"They'll want to know why we waited."

"I could tell them it was because I didn't trust no one but this guy I know, but they'd probably say we was protecting your cousin."

"What difference does it make? He's gone and there won't be any more murders."

"Wish I was sure of that as you."

"Daniel?" Sarah Ann's voice was small, sounding far away. "Daniel? Are you all right?"

"C'mon down, it's okay."

She started down as Daniel got up off the couch and walked over to meet her at the bottom of the stairs. She stopped halfway, her eyes popping wide as she saw A.L. looming huge and tall, stooped slightly over his crutches.

"It's okay, honey," Daniel said. "That's Mr. Smith from upstairs."

"What happened?"

"C'mon over and sit down." Daniel took her hand and led her to the couch. He sat next to her, half turned, his arm behind her. "It was Billy," he said.

"Oh, God, I knew it. I just knew it."

"It's all right. He's gone and he won't be back."

"Oh, God, Daniel, what if he had—"

"He didn't. That's all. He didn't."

A.L. shifted his weight, straightening up so he could walk.

Daniel stood up. "Could I get you a beer or something?"

"No. No thanks. Maybe some other time. Doctor says I got to keep off this leg and get lots of rest if it's ever gonna heal." He smiled and shook the hand Daniel offered. "We can talk some more tomorrow about going to the cops."

Daniel nodded. "All right," he said, "and thanks again."

"Nothing to it. Maybe you can do the same for me some time."

"Okay."

Outside, far off toward the center of the city, they could hear the police sirens, first close and then up on Vine Street. A.L. and Daniel listened until they were sure the sirens were headed for the rail yards.

"Could be anything," A.L. said.

Daniel nodded.

30

BILLY CROUCHED in the dark corner of the boxcar, listening for more shouting. When it did not come he crept toward the door and looked out. He heard the shout again, and back along the train, near the end, he could see smoke and the bright lash of fire crawling over the embankment.

He wondered where the train was headed and whether this empty car was going all the way to Charlotte. He decided to find out now while the train was still going slow. He stood in the frame of the doorway, leaped up, and grabbed the upper molding strip, pumping his legs, swinging back into the car and out over the ground. He pumped twice, three times, feeling his hold loosening and then at the last second he pumped hard and swung up onto the top of the car.

At first he found it hard to stand against the sway of the train, and when he tried to walk his legs threatened to give out and send him toppling over the edge. But gradually he found the rhythm and then it was easy. He was about halfway back, and he decided to check the front of the train first.

It was picking up speed now, and the sway had become a jolting lurch, making it even harder to walk. When he had to cross from car to car the clang of the couplings was deafening, and he moved with extra care.

Every car he tried was marked for New York City. He got as close to the engine as he dared and then began working his way back, beginning to feel just an edge of panic at not finding even one that was going south.

He grabbed the rounded loops of the ladder at the top of a large green boxcar and eased himself over the edge. Halfway down, he leaped out onto a flat car that had two great canvas lumps in the middle. He checked the tag on the front: Atlanta. He had been so busy looking for Charlotte that he almost had not seen it.

He walked over and lifted the edge of the canvas and slid on under. It was a lot better place than an empty car. There was enough room in the middle under the machine to lie down and stretch out.

The train was moving fast now, and the loud droning rumble seemed a safe and familiar sound. Billy began to relax and to think about Georgia.

He would stay long enough, he decided, to get his dogs and his rifle and then he would head up into Tennessee, into the high mountains. Nobody would come after him there and he could spend his days the way he had before, hunting and fishing. Maybe he could even grow himself a garden.

He could not understand why Daniel had ever left home.